DONNA VANLIERE'S NOVELS ARE:

"Magical."
—*BookPage*

"Touching and uplifting."
—*Library Journal*

"Compelling."
—*American Profile*

"Heart-tugging."
—*Publishers Weekly*

"Truly superb."
—Medina County *Gazette*

"Delightful."
—*The Tampa Tribune* and *Times*

"Heartwarming."
—*The Sanford Herald*

"Full of precious gifts for all of us."
—*The Washington Times*

Also by
DONNA VANLIERE

THE CHRISTMAS SHOES

THE CHRISTMAS BLESSING

THE CHRISTMAS HOPE

The Angels of Morgan Hill

DONNA VANLIERE

St. Martin's Paperbacks

This is a work of fiction. All of the characters, organizations, and events portrayed in this novel are either products of the author's imagination or are used fictitiously.

THE ANGELS OF MORGAN HILL

Copyright © 2006 by Donna VanLiere.
Excerpt from *The Christmas Promise* copyright © 2007 by Donna VanLiere.

Library of Congress Catalog Card Number: 2006040637

ISBN: 0-312-93379-7
EAN: 978-0-312-93379-1

Printed in the United States of America

St. Martin's Press hardcover edition / October 2006
St. Martin's Paperbacks edition / December 2007

St. Martin's Paperbacks are published by St. Martin's Press, 175 Fifth Avenue, New York, NY 10010.

10 9 8 7 6 5 4 3 2 1

For my mother, Alice Jane Payne
who grew up in a place like Morgan Hill

ACKNOWLEDGMENTS

Much appreciation and thanks to . . .

Troy, Gracie, and Kate for being the sweetest part of my life.

My mother for inspiring this story. Many years ago she told me that she was nearly a grown woman before she ever saw a black person up close. She and my father, Archie, grew up in Greene County, Tennessee, and many of their childhood tales of walking down railroad tracks, milking cows, growing tobacco, and spending time in small country stores like Henry's are reflected in these pages.

Jennifer Gates and Esmond Harmsworth for reading this book over and over and then over again. It wouldn't be the book it is today without your input!

Jennifer Enderlin for believing in Morgan Hill and inspiring that belief in others! Welcome, June!! Thanks to Sally Richardson, George Witte, Matthew Shear, John Karle, Matthew Baldacci, Mike Storrings (for the beautiful cover), and the entire sales staff at St. Martin's for making it happen.

My aunt Geraldine Culberson for being my chauffeur as I traveled through Greene County. Thanks to my aunt Maxine Harrison and her husband, Merrill, for providing a place to stay and lots of great meals!

I met Rhonda Julian in her home as her four small children played nearby. Rhonda invited her father, Jack Lawson, and uncle Tom Lawson over to talk about raising tobacco in the 1940s. She was kind and gracious, and it was obvious her children adored her. Leukemia took her from this world much too early (her father also passed away during the writing of this book), but I'm grateful for the spirit in which she welcomed me and the belief she had in this story.

James "Spud" Ailshie, a former general store owner (and tobacco farmer!) from the 1940s who made Henry's store come to life within these pages.

My pastor, Chris Carter, and everyone at the Orchard Church in Franklin for friendship and continued inspiration.

I started writing this book a few years ago at the log cabin home of Johnny and Janet Hunt, Raymond and Glenda Pumphrey, and Jim and Kathy Law. Thank you all for the ideal setting!

"Miss" Karen Parente, "Miss" Carole Consiglio, and "Miss" Kelly Long at Little School for your heart!

And again, to Bailey, who does whatever he can to always be by my side.

I am a part of all that I have met.
—ALFRED TENNYSON, "ULYSSES"

PROLOGUE

It was raining real hard the day we buried my daddy. Mama said it was because the angels were crying; but after hours of drenching downpour I doubted the angels were crying tears of joy about seeing Daddy in heaven but instead were just downright upset about having him there.

My father was a diabetic and a drunk—two conditions that don't get along well with each other. Doc Langley kept telling him the drinking was going to kill him but Daddy never listened. He was playing cards with Beef, Dewey, and the rest of the boys one night when he had what they described as "some sort of fit" and passed out. They thought he'd just drunk too much so they let him be, head down on the table for the next twelve hours while they finished their game. By the time one of the boys got the good sense to think Daddy wasn't taking a catnap (trust me when I say that taking just twelve hours to figure something out was a record-breaking feat for them), they fetched the doctor, but Daddy was all but gone. Doc said it wouldn't have done any good if he'd gotten to him earlier—the alcohol poisoned his bloodstream and threw him into a diabetic coma. He was twenty-eight years old. I was nine.

The day we buried him was the same day I first saw a black face up close. East Tennessee didn't have slaves during the Civil War, so there was never a large population of black people to settle there. Many lived in Greeneville but in my nine years of life I'd never set foot anywhere but Morgan Hill. My brother, John, and I were riding in the car with Aunt Dora when we got behind an old pickup. Aunt Dora was looking for a way to pass when a tiny head popped up from inside the truck bed. He was a little boy, no older than John, and the color of pure milk chocolate. His head was round and bald and his eyes were as big and black as shiny marbles. He hung on to the tailgate and stared at us. I remembered hearing Mama talk about some coloreds who had moved to town but I'd never seen them, and in that brief moment I found myself gawking at him. He almost lost his footing when the truck lunged over a rut in the road and, as suddenly as he appeared, the little boy smiled real big—the biggest, whitest smile I'd ever seen—and ducked down into the truck before it pulled onto the drive that led to the Cannon farm.

"Well, look at that," Aunt Dora said. "There's them coloreds your mama said moved to town. They should shake things up." I didn't really know what she meant at the time but all that would change soon enough.

That was the spring of 1947 in Morgan Hill, Tennessee. Morgan Hill is fifty-five miles northeast of Knoxville where it lays claim to the most beautiful rolling green hills you'll ever see. Thomas Morgan was the first to settle there in 1810. He lived at the base of a small hill he deemed Morgan's Hill in honor of himself. The *s* was eventually dropped. Who knows why. In 1947 Morgan Hill boasted Walker's (a tiny general market with a single gas pump in front), the Morgan Hill Baptist Church, and the Langley School Building (named after Doc Langley's great granddaddy), which housed grades one through

twelve in one hot, cramped brick building on top
of the hill right in the middle of town. We were a
poor community; some of the homes, ours in-
cluded, that were hooked to electricity just three
years earlier couldn't afford the electric bill so we
continued to use coal oil lamps. We milked our
own cows, butchered our own pigs, grew our
own vegetables, and scraped out a living the best
we knew how.

Now you might think that what you're about
to read has a great deal to do with my father and
growing up poor in east Tennessee, but there is
so much more—what captured my heart was the
hope of belonging and the dream of family. Fifty-
four years have passed and many of the details
have blurred, but the memories of the heart are
as alive for me today as they were then. The
woman I am has a great deal to do with that
ninth year of my life. It started out as any other
year, nothing extraordinary, but as each day un-
folded it became remarkable in every way. There
are times when I'm still amazed that we made it
through. It has been said that every life has a
story. This is my story, although it belongs to so
many others, for I was never alone. They were always with me . . . and still are today.

Chapter
ONE

The Morgan Hill cemetery was right behind the church, so you can imagine how convenient funerals were at that time. After a message by the preacher, we would simply walk out the back door and say good-bye to the poor dead soul in the casket. On a day of rain, we'd have the funeral service in the church and leave the casket there until the rain let up; at that time the undertakers would come back and bury it. But an eleven o'clock wedding was scheduled on the day we buried Daddy, and apparently the bride did not want his casket up front with her as she exchanged vows with her beloved.

Never in the history of the Morgan Hill Baptist Church had it ever been double booked. The funeral was scheduled for ten o'clock but the rain kept folks in their homes. It was close to ten-thirty when the first mourners arrived, and the bride and her mother had already beautified our tiny building by hanging construction paper bells and hearts at the front of the church. A big red banner that read "Naomi and Cal Forever" was draped over the preaching podium—nice for a wedding, but not exactly proper send-off decorations for a dead man. A handful of mourners sloshed their way into the church. Poor Naomi was beside herself.

"Mama, there is a dead man layin' here at the altar!" she sobbed. "He is goin' to ruin my weddin'!" Naomi's mother patted and cooed and soothed the best she knew how and greeted the smattering of early wedding guests that trickled through the door with a big, toothy smile as she corralled them to the back pews until further notice.

It was decided we would have to hold the service in the cemetery, but everyone wanted to wait till the rain slowed down to just a drizzle. So to stall for time we sang a few of the hymns that were sung at everybody's funeral. First we sang "In the Sweet Bye and Bye." The rain kept coming. Naomi kept wailing. Then we sang "Shall We Gather at the River," and, by the sight of the water now standing in the cemetery, it seemed we would indeed be gathering at the river very soon. We waited and waited and sang and sang, and the longer we waited and the louder we sang, the more nervous Naomi and her mother became.

We all made a mad dash to the gravesite, praying that the leaves on the trees would somehow keep us dry. They didn't. We stood like drowned rats huddled around a four-by-seven hole trying to act sad as water soaked clear through to our underpants. Our preacher for the past thirty years had retired, so Mama asked Pete Fletcher if he'd conduct Daddy's funeral. Pete wasn't a preacher, he was a farmer and mechanic, and I thought he'd come close to passing out at the thought of sending a dead man to his earthly resting place. Pete tried his best to talk about hope in the resurrection of Christ and being with Daddy again in heaven someday, but to be honest we were all too waterlogged to listen. Four men lowered the casket, the grave straps soggy and slippery in their hands, causing the box to slip and bang, then fall to the bottom with a wet thud. Not one of Morgan Hill's most touching funerals, but certainly one of the most memorable.

Mama made my seven-year-old brother, John, and me ride with Aunt Dora back to our house. She was Daddy's only sister and drove all the way from Cleveland, Ohio, for the funeral. Dora was thirty and had fat knees, thick ankles, and a bad case of being hopelessly single. When a single man, regardless of age or lack of teeth, was anywhere near, she wrapped her fat, sausage arms around John's neck pretending to be the consummate mothering type. John said he couldn't wait for her to go back to "Ohi" as soon as possible. But if we hadn't ridden with Aunt Dora, I wouldn't have the memory of Milo's little black face in the back of that beat-up truck etched in my mind today.

We lived in a tiny white farmhouse where Mama had been born. It had two bedrooms and a porch that wrapped around two sides of it. The front of the house faced the railroad tracks, which didn't make any sense because unless you were walking along the tracks or riding on the train, no one ever saw the front of the house. Our main entrance was off the kitchen at the back of the house, which faced the driveway. I was three years old when we moved in. I don't remember where we lived before that, but Mama always said it wasn't fit for a mean-tailed dog. I put on some dry clothes while the adults scrambled and fussed and flew around the kitchen, spreading out enough food to feed all of us, *plus* Naomi and Cal's wedding reception guests. I fixed a plate and snuck out to the porch with John following behind. One night two years earlier, after Daddy threw Mama into a wall, John became convinced the bogeyman was in our house, under his bed to be exact. I checked under his bed every night. When John learned to talk he had a stammer. He'd get caught on a word and sound like a tractor engine starting in winter. "B-b-b-b-but," he'd sputter. As he got older the stuttering faded but I always knew when he was afraid because words came hard for him then. If it was just Mama, John, and me at the house he could talk fine, but if Daddy came home it would take John forever to spit something out. Since Daddy died John hadn't stammered one time.

John didn't change out of his wet clothes and that galled Mama to no end. "John Charles. Don't you have enough gumption to get out of them wet clothes?" I never knew if it was really a lack of gumption that bothered Mama, or if it was the fact that John had mannerisms that reminded her of Daddy. Whatever the reason she was determined to give him an extra dose.

"They don't bother me, Mama. They ain't that wet."

"The water's running down your legs and squishing out between your toes," she said, pointing to the foot-shaped wet spot on the porch.

John slapped his foot to make another soggy print. "I know. I like it!" Mama rolled her eyes, mumbling something about John not having the gumption God gave a bump on a log, and walked back into the house. Since we'd heard the gumption speech a hundred times before, we dove into our plates and ate like pigs. We watched the rain pour off the front of the porch, stuck our feet under the waterfall that was flowing off the overhang, and never once mentioned Daddy—not that we didn't want to; we just didn't know what to say. Sadness for his passing never occurred to us.

Daddy worked as a carpenter (although you'd be hard-pressed to actually find someone who saw as much as a hammer in his hand) and his work took him out of town for weeks at a time. He would often go into Knoxville with Beef and a couple of the boys for work, but somewhere between Knoxville and home the money would be all but gone. Whatever money he hadn't guzzled or gambled was given to Mama. She'd learned years earlier not to badger him for it because that only made him angry. He was scrawny but he was fast and could lay her out cold with one quick, hard whack with the back of his hand. Mama knew not to fight with him. When he'd hand over what little cash he had left, she'd just take it from him real easy and then sneak away and hide it in a coffee can she kept buried in the backyard.

They married on May 6, 1937, the same day the Hindenburg exploded. Mama would say years later that their marriage "was as doomed as that gigantic blimp." I arrived nine months later to very little, if any, fanfare. (By that time Mama knew what she'd gotten herself into and adding another life to a home shared with Daddy wasn't exactly a reason for celebration.) When Mama was young she was smart, funny, and pretty with long chestnut hair, blue eyes, a fine-drawn face, and China doll skin. She walked to school every morning with her best friend, Margaret, and a boy named Joe Cannon. Margaret used to tease my mother that Joe was sweet on her but if that was true Joe never did anything about it. He was too shy and backward to do anything more than walk to and from school with her. As people in the community would always say, nobody ever knew "how pretty Francine Parker ever ended up with Lonnie Gable." Even then, my daddy was a cocky, scrawny know-it-all who appeared to be on the fast track to nowhere.

Mama had lost her own mother six years earlier so who knows, maybe if her mother had been around she wouldn't have been craving the attention Daddy gave her and run off with him after graduation. But Mama was never one for getting into a mess and then looking to somebody else to get her out of it. I think she probably hoped Daddy would just leave on one of his "jobs" and never come home, but that never happened. I think she saw his death as freedom from a whole lot of trouble.

John and I stayed quiet on the porch and gobbled down lemon pie, chocolate pie, and German chocolate cake like survivors of a POW camp, but if anybody came out on the porch we'd bring the food to our mouths, look real sad, and sigh. Every now and then Mama peeked her head out the door and we looked up at her with pitiful hound-dog eyes. "Jane, are you and John getting enough to eat?" We nodded our heads, glancing at our plates that looked as if they'd been picked over by vultures. It seemed a pathetic act but if it brought her some sort of peace to think that we were indeed sad in spirit over Daddy's passing then we'd play along.

Aunt Dora popped her fat face out the door above Mama's and said, "Your daddy's with the angels." We nodded again and looked somber as she and Mama closed the screen door behind them.

Henry didn't pretend though. Henry Walker had three grown children, fine tufts of hair at the top of his balding head that blew in the wind like the feathers of a baby bird, and a heart bigger than anybody I'd ever known. He'd tell John and me the greatest stories we'd ever heard. Our favorite was of the Three Musketeers. We never knew if he was making most of the story up, but we always believed that we were two of the three musketeers saving women and children from peril.

"I'm gonna write a book someday," I would tell Henry. "And you'll be in it."

"Make sure you tell people how good looking I am," he would always say.

Mama didn't like me to talk about it. "There's work to do, Jane," she'd say. "You can't work while you're dreaming." I learned to keep my book ideas for Henry since he was my best friend.

Henry never said things like "Jane, your daddy sure did love you" or "Jane, you were the apple in your daddy's eye" as so many other people did. He walked onto the porch, gave me one of his great big bear hugs—one that made me feel like I was being squeezed by Heaven itself, and said, "Hey, Pretty Girl." He always called me Pretty Girl although that was far from accurate. I could see myself in the mirror; I knew what I looked like—I was as plain as my name. I had thin, uneven, short brown hair from the haircuts that Mama gave me, ears that stuck out like wing nuts, and freckles across my nose. I was common and ungraceful, a far cry from pretty, but somehow when Henry called me Pretty Girl I believed him.

"We saw them coloreds that moved to town," I said.

"They got 'em a scrawny little colored boy no older than me," John said. "He's got great big eyes and a pitiful, hound-dog face."

"He don't look like that no how," I said. "What're they doing out at the Cannons', Henry?"

"Helping put out their tobacco."

"What do colored folk eat?" John said. He always could ask the dumbest questions.

"They eat what we eat," Henry said.

"What do they smell like?"

"What kind of fool question is that?" I said. "They smell like people!"

"Aunt Dora says they're gonna shake things up," John said. "How they gonna shake things up, Henry?" That was a legitimate question.

"I don't know," Henry said. But I could tell by the way he looked at us that Henry did know what Aunt Dora meant. He just didn't want to talk about it. He put his arm around my shoulder. "I sure am sorry you lost your father, Jane."

For the first time all day I realized that maybe I should be sad. Not that my daddy had died, but that I'd never really had one in the first place. When I looked at Henry I realized he knew all about my daddy, even things that I didn't know. It struck me that somebody who walked on this earth for twenty-eight years wasn't even missed in death . . . not even by his own family.

When Henry and his wife, Loretta, were ready to leave, Henry found Fran in the barn getting the cans ready for milking. It was just past noon, way too early to worry about the evening milking. Henry knew she was trying to get away from everyone in the house. He was struck by her appearance. *When did Frannie get that old?* he thought, remembering the little girl who used to giggle when he'd pretend to pull a nickel out of her ear. "Need help, Fran?" She was deaf in one ear from a childhood fever and hadn't heard him. He stepped in front of her and she jumped, wiping her eyes.

"Good Lord, Henry!" She hurried past him and picked up a milking stool for him to sit. "Did you eat?"

"Did I eat?" He patted his belly. "I ate enough for ten men." Henry watched as she grabbed a piece of rope and played with it, twisting it till her knuckles were stretched white. There was an unwritten code in the hills of Tennessee that said you couldn't ask for help, you couldn't share a true feeling, and you could never, ever wear your heart on your sleeve. Henry knew the code but he was always the first person to ignore it, especially with somebody he'd known as long as Fran. "How you doing, Fran?" He reached for another milking stool and set it down next to him, patting it for her to sit.

She didn't look at him. She couldn't. "Good," she whispered, sitting on the steps leading to the barn loft.

She looked uncomfortable. Henry leaned forward, tilting his head to see her eyes. "Fran?" A single tear rolled down her face but she remained quiet, winding the rope around a finger. He got up and patted her leg so he could be on her right side where she could hear him best. He sat next to her on the step. "I know you don't believe it right now but everything's going to be all right, Frannie." More silent tears spilled onto her hands.

She shook her head. "You don't know how many times I've relived the day Lonnie said we'd get married. In my head I don't run off and marry him, Henry. I never, ever marry him." She looked up into the rafters. Her voice was breaking. "I don't know what I'm going to do."

Henry leaned her head on his shoulder, wrapping his arm around her. There was always a sense of hope when Henry was near. "It's all right, Fran. Everything's gonna be all right." For the longest time he just sat while she cried.

"I think I wanted him to die," she whispered, wiping her face. "I'd lie awake at night and wish he'd never open the door again . . . but he would. He'd be gone for days, even weeks at a time before falling through the door. I'd lay real still, hoping he'd think I was asleep but it didn't matter to him. He'd smell like liquor and sweat and I swear I hated him, Henry. I hated his smell and I hated his hands on me and I hated him for laying with other women and then forcing himself on me." She pressed the palms of her hands into her thighs and rubbed them up and down her legs. "Why did I marry him, Henry? What was wrong with me?" She pressed harder into her legs. "So many times I—just—wished—he'd—die."

Henry noticed the lines around her mouth and the dark sunken patches under her eyes. Ten years with Lonnie had been hard on her. "Fran, your wishing didn't kill Lonnie," he said. "Years of hard drinking and bad decisions killed him."

A steady stream of tears fell off her chin. "I'm pregnant, Henry." He looked long and hard at her. "You look as baffled as I am."

"Are you sure, Fran?"

She nodded and wiped her eyes. "I'm sure."

"It could be the stomach sickness. Lottie's kids were all down with it last week."

"No. It's not that. I've been sick for a few weeks now and I got sick again last night after eating supper and then this morning before the funeral."

"Well, it could be something you ate that had gone bad." He glanced up to see Loretta step inside the barn. She stood at the door and stopped.

"Every time I throw up I'm brought right back to the times I carried Jane and John," she said.

"It's the same kind of sick." She leaned forward and wept into her hands. "What am I going to do? I can't have another baby."

Loretta knelt in front of her. "Who knows what one little baby will grow up to be? Why, this baby could grow up to find a cure for polio." Fran didn't move. "One day they're just a squawling, demanding little thing and the next thing you know they're leading a country through war like Roosevelt or Churchill." Loretta looked in Fran's eyes. "A new little life always brings so much hope with it when it comes into the world." Fran always liked Loretta. She had married Henry ten years earlier. Her husband had died in a mining explosion in Kentucky, and Edith, Henry's first wife, had died five years before that. Loretta stopped in Morgan Hill for gas on the way to visit a sister. She had no idea she'd find a husband stacking chicken feed at the general store. Loretta had dark auburn hair and a face that she said was crowded with freckles and those were being pushed around by wrinkles. She reminded Fran of her own mother in so many ways; and although she was trying, Loretta was wrong about this— another baby meant no hope at all.

"Fran, this probably ain't the best time to

bring this up," Henry said, "but I came out here to ask if you'd be willing to help me in the store for the next few days."

She looked up at him. "You ain't never needed much help before."

Henry stood and shuffled his feet on the barn floor. "Loretta's been down in her back and this morning it was worse." Fran looked at Loretta.

"I ain't got no business slinging a bag of feed on my back anymore. I felt something go snap and have been in misery since." Fran searched her face. Loretta knew Fran would never take the job if she thought they were handing out charity to her.

"The last time I threw my back out we got Mavis Duke to help," Loretta said.

"Don't ask that wheezing Mavis Duke," Henry said. "The last time she helped me do inventory I thought a cat was dying in the stock room."

Fran blew her nose into the handkerchief. "All right, Henry."

He smiled, hoping for something to say, but he couldn't find the words because Henry knew this was not a good situation. Not a good situation at all.

That night Aunt Dora stayed in the room that I shared with John, which frustrated me to no end.

I didn't know why she came for the funeral. Her mama died when she and Daddy were little, and Dora went to live in Ohio with an aunt while my grandpa raised Daddy. She hadn't seen my father in years.

After watching her spread cold cream onto her pale, doughy face, I knew I couldn't stand by and watch as she made her way down those sausage arms and beefy legs, so I opted to sleep on the floor in the front room with John. Somehow the thought of sleeping on a hardwood floor and possibly being peed on was better than the image of that greasy puss coming toward me with a goodnight kiss.

We heard Mama in the kitchen arranging leftover food in the icebox, throwing scraps in the slop bucket, and washing up empty platters and bowls. John and I laid in silence, listening to her work. For as long as I could remember it had always been Mama, me, and John. I'd have given anything to find a daddy, a real one that liked us and didn't hit Mama. I guess every kid has a moment when they want to run away; they throw a stuffed toy into a suitcase and sit on the front stoop or maybe even make it as far as the end of the driveway. I thought of it often because I knew there had to be a better place for us to live, a place where we could be a real family, and I was determined to find that place. I reached over in the dark and held on to John's hand as we listened to Mama move about the kitchen. We didn't bother her. We didn't even offer to help because she wouldn't have wanted it; it wasn't her way. It's not that we were at odds with our mother but there was an untouchable sadness to Mama, and John and I always knew when she wanted to be alone. I stayed awake for the longest time studying on where we could find a daddy so we could become a real family but I was too tired to think and drifted off to sleep to the rhythmic sound of crickets in our backyard and the slight tinkling of Mama's spoon sloshing round and round in her coffee cup.

I stumbled my way to the kitchen the next morning. Mama looked weary. I don't know if she ever went to bed. "Jane, get your Aunt Dora up for breakfast."

I walked to the bedroom door and knocked. "Aunt Dora. It's time for breakfast." She didn't answer. I knocked again, louder this time. Mama hated us to be late for breakfast. "Aunt Dora! Wake up!"

Her feet slapped the floor until the door opened. John and I gasped at the sight; her sagging bosoms swayed in shocking reality. "Be right there," she said, yawning, and tapped my nose.

John and I folded the blankets before rushing to the kitchen. Aunt Dora was right behind us, her bosoms hoisted into place.

After breakfast John loaded Aunt Dora's suitcase into her trunk. We lied about how much we'd miss her and turned to walk back to the house. "Aren't you going to come over here and give me some sugar?" It echoed through our frightened ears. *Give me some sugar. Give me some sugar.* I pushed John forward and he dug his heels into the gravel.

"You all act like you've got some sense and get over there and give your Aunt Dora some sugar," Mama said.

The ultimate wish of any kid is, if they have to endure a kiss of any kind, that it be quick and to the cheek. But the worst kiss of all, the one every kid has dreaded from the beginning of time, is the full-mouth contact kiss. That's a hard one to bounce back from.

Poor John. The kiss came fast, a firm yet moist arrow that left a bright red ring around his mouth. He reeled backward. Aunt Dora's arms reached for me. "Good-bye, Janie Girl Baby Doll." I made my move, a quick quarter-inch turn of the face that sealed for me a lip-cheek combo. I lifted my hand and wiggled my fingers in a feeble attempt to wave good-bye as she drove away.

"Good riddance," John said, wiping his mouth.

"Come on," Mama said. "We've already missed Sunday school. Let's get ready for church."

I'd been wearing the same dress to church for two years. Somebody made it out of a flour sack (even women's dresses were made out of flour sacks) and handed it down to me when I was seven and it was way too big then. Now it was way too small, riding up above my knees. "Put that dress on and hush," Mama said. "You wear them old overalls so much you're gonna turn into a boy." I slipped the dress over my head and looked at my arms that hung a good four inches past the cuffs of the sleeves and prayed that the dress would fall apart the next time we washed it.

Fran always sat in the same pew: the third one back from the front on the right-hand side. The pews were hard and rough in spots. The walls were white and despite the dreariness of the day, the sun shone through the long windows on each side, bathing the poplar wood cross and the pews with golden circles of light. Fran's friend Margaret came in and sat right behind her. Her family had been sitting behind Fran as long as anyone could remember. Margaret was Fran's age and although she was heavier she looked younger than Fran, with tawny skin and silky, flax-colored hair she kept knotted behind and held in place with bobby pins. "How you doing, Frannie?" Margaret asked.

"Doing good." In the South, if you were laid up in the hospital dying and somebody asked how you were doing, you always said, "Doing good. Doing real good."

Fran and Margaret had known each other since they were young girls and they always acted more like sisters than friends. Margaret turned around to watch for her husband and smiled at Joe Cannon who was standing at the back of the church. Joe had wavy dark blond hair, deep brown eyes, a straight nose and blunt chin, and skin that turned the color of coffee with cream in it during the summer. Margaret leaned in close to Fran's ear. "Can't you see when a man is looking at you?"

Fran folded her arms. "I suppose I can. I have eyes."

Margaret laughed. "Well, they don't seem to be working."

"What in the world are you talking about?"

Margaret cast her eyes to the back of the building. "Joe Cannon is standing at the back of the church and was looking right at you."

"Well, of course he looked at me. There ain't but five of us in here. Is he blind?"

"I'm sitting here, too, but he wasn't looking at me no how!"

Fran reached behind her and swatted at Margaret. "Hush up. That ain't fit for church talk."

"Your face is flushed, Fran Gable."

"Well, of course it is. I'm sitting here in church and listening to foolishness."

"There was a time when you were sweet on him."

"That was so many years ago that I can't even remember how old we were."

"Well, he's back from Atlanta for a while and he's looking at you again so you better be looking at him!"

Fran snapped her head to look at her. "Have you gone mad?" Margaret leaned forward in her pew and grabbed hold of Fran's arm, laughing. "You are crazy, Margaret Davies. Let me go." She yanked her arm from Margaret's grasp. "This ain't no way to act on Sunday!" She tried to be mad but when she looked at Margaret she snickered. She knew the laughs would soon end. If Joe was looking at her it would all change in a couple of months when her belly protruded.

John and I always waited to the last possible minute to sit down, so when Ida Carpenter started to pound on the piano keys we took our place next to Mama. "Hi, Miss Jane," Margaret said. "That sure is a pretty dress you have on." I cringed. She sure wasn't helping my cause. "Well, who in the world is that?" We turned around and saw the biggest, blackest man I'd ever seen standing at the back of the church with the Cannons. The little colored boy from the back of the pickup truck stood next to him.

"Daggum," John said. "There's a giant in church!"

The congregation grew quiet as everybody turned to look. The colored woman held a little girl tight to her chest. She looked no older than three and her hair was tied with strips of red cloth in tiny braids that stuck up all over her head. Her small black hands were the size of a baby doll's. I thought she was the most beautiful child I'd ever seen. I heard Margaret mumble something about them "having their own churches" under her breath behind me and then,

"Joe Cannon knows better than to bring them here."

Mama turned to look at her. "Where're they supposed to go, Margaret? There ain't no colored church close to here." Mama caught the woman's eye and she smiled, looking at the floor. Mama got up and Margaret grabbed her hand.

"Sit on down, Fran."

Mama stared at her and drew her hand away before walking to the colored family. It was unlike my mother. She was never the first to greet anybody. But something moved her that day—something picked her right up out of her seat and drew her to a mother clinging to her child. Everybody in the congregation stopped to watch.

She shook the woman's hand. "You must be Addy and Willie Dean." She put her arm around Addy and walked her to our pew. "We heard that you were in town." I looked at many of our friends, those who had filled our home after Daddy's funeral just the day before, and they were clearly not happy with Mama, with the Cannons, or with God Himself for that matter.

Joe Cannon was twenty-two years old when he was sent to Europe to fight in the war. Like many Southern men, he could aim a gun with a steady hand and shoot any moving target without breaking a sweat. Since he'd been through war he wasn't about to let the quiet of the church unsettle him. "Come on in," he said, ushering the colored man to the pew. My mouth dropped open when the enormous figure walked past me.

Henry and some of the other men had asked Pete Fletcher if he'd preach at church for the next few Sundays. He was sitting in the front pew preparing his message and said later that he could feel the hairs stand up on the back of his neck as silence covered the church. He turned around and saw the four colored faces that had brought the congregation to a standstill.

"Good morning," he said, rising out of his pew and extending his hand. "I'm Pete Fletcher."

The colored man kept his head low when he answered. "Willie Dean Turner."

Pete looked out at the congregation and cleared his throat. He was a thin, hard-muscled man of thirty with a shock of unruly brown hair that always looked as if it'd fly off his head in a heavy wind. "We've got some new friends with us today." His voice was weak. Many people shifted in their seats, looking at the floor. "The Turners have moved here and are working out at the Cannons'. I just wanted to let them know how happy we are to have them with us today." John began to clap but nobody followed. You could have driven a team of horses through the middle of the quiet. It was one of those quiets where the smallest sound, like a scratch or someone swallowing, is noisy. Henry and Loretta jumped up from their pew and sprang to the Turners' side.

"Glad to meet you, Willie Dean," Henry said, shaking his hand. "I've been meaning to come out to the farm to see you."

"Mornin', Addy," Loretta said. "I'm Loretta Walker." Addy smiled and whispered hello. "You come see us any time or just let me know anything you need and I'll get it out to you."

Henry knelt down to Milo and whispered in his ear. "You come on down to the store and I'll give you an ice-cold CoCola." Milo nodded and buried the side of his head in his daddy's arm. Otis and Nona Dodd, the shortest and oldest people in Morgan Hill, shuffled out of their seats and I watched as Nona's hand disappeared in the giant black hand.

Margaret didn't seem happy at all and her heavy sigh landed hot and humid on the back of my neck, but since Otis and Nona were as old as Moses and Zipporah themselves they didn't pay attention to her or anybody else as they made their way back to their pew.

"What's everybody so quiet for?" John asked Mama. She raised a finger to her lips to hush him. I looked around the congregation and wondered if this is what Aunt Dora meant when she said the colored family would "shake things up"?

I didn't hear a word Pete said that day but I never took my eyes off him. Something was happening in our church that I'd never felt before. I didn't know what it was but I knew I didn't like it. Some people went out of their way to make the Turners feel welcome, talking and laughing with them after the service, but some people, people like Margaret, left without a word.

When the service ended John and I hid behind Henry's truck, content to stay far away from Willie Dean until Henry's outstretched arm struck fear in both of us.

"Come here, Jane," he said. "John, come meet the Turners before they leave." I felt John push me from behind and I stumbled toward Henry. The man looming in front of me became bigger with each step I took. "This is Jane and John."

"They're my youngins," Mama said to Addy.

Henry looked at us. "Willie Dean and his family came all the way from Mississippi to help the Cannons on the farm." When Joe got back from the war he went to work in a textile plant in Atlanta owned by a war buddy's father. Joe was the youngest in a family of six and the only surviving son. Two older brothers, Del Jr. and Ludlow, died many years earlier. Joe's father, Del, wasn't aging gracefully; few men who worked long, hot hours on farms in the South did. Helen said that as Del got older he seemed to be losing his wits. In late 1946 Joe sent a message to relatives in Alabama and Mississippi to spread the word that Del would sell off part of the land to anybody willing to come work it with him. Willie Dean Turner was the first to answer, and Joe came home from Atlanta long enough to help put out the tobacco.

"Shake Willie Dean's hand," Henry said. We didn't move.

Mama leaned in to my ear. "Act like you've got some sense and go shake that man's hand." But I couldn't do it. Neither could John. We both stood frozen. Then Willie Dean bent over and stuck out his hand in front of me. I felt my hand rise and watched as it disappeared in the mass of coal black flesh. He shook John's hand and, as usual, John couldn't keep his mouth shut.

"Holy cow," he shouted. "You're as big as a horse!" Henry laughed and Mama twisted John's ear, which made Henry laugh harder.

The little girl reached for her daddy's hands and began pulling herself up his legs. Willie Dean pushed her onto his shoulders. "Can you reach them, Baby?" She stretched out her arms toward the sky.

"Higher," she said.

He grabbed her hands and helped her stand on his shoulders. She stretched her tiny hands, reaching for the heavens, waving them around in the air. "There they are," she said, squealing. "I'm touching them. I'm touching the angels." I watched them and wished I could find a dad like that for John and me, one who would let us crawl over him and sit us on top of his shoulders.

The colored boy ran and picked up a scruffy-haired three-legged dog and put him in the truck bed. "Where'd you ever find a dog that ugly?" John asked.

"He found us," the boy said. "Daddy said since he went to all the trouble of finding us, the least we could do is feed him." The dog wagged his tail and buried his nose under the boy's arm.

"What's his name?" I asked, patting the dog's back.

"He's Fred Dog," a small bird-like voice chirped behind me. I helped the little girl as she climbed into the truck.

"You're the blackest boy I've ever seen," John said.

"You're the whitest one *I've* ever seen," the boy said.

"What's your name?" I asked.

"What's *your* name?"

"I asked you first."

"Yeah, she asked you first," John said.

We stared at one another a good long time before the boy stuck out his hand to us, just like his daddy had done. "I'm Milo Isaiah Turner." I shook his hand and then John shook it with a nice, firm squeeze, bouncing it up and down for effect.

"I'm John Charles Gable." He sounded like a man applying for a job. He pointed at me with his thumb. "This is Jane."

"That's Rose," Milo said.

That was that. We'd officially met the first black people we'd ever seen. We watched as they drove away. Milo peered over the tailgate, just like he'd done the first time we saw him, and he waved at us, a big, floppy wave to make sure we saw him. John and I waved back, wondering what it was going to be like to have a colored boy as a friend.

We were quiet on our walk home. John and I teetered in silence atop the rails. "Mama, why didn't some of them people talk to the Turners?" I asked.

"Some people are just like that, Jane."

That wasn't an answer. "But they acted like they didn't like them and they don't even know them." She was quiet. "Why you reckon they acted like they didn't like them?"

She sighed. "I don't *know*, Jane. Some people are strange that way and that's just the way it is." When *that's just the way it is* was spoken in the South it meant that the conversation was over. It wasn't an answer either but I knew Mama didn't want to talk about it. I wanted to ask her more questions. I wanted to ask her why people wouldn't even look at the Turners or why some of our oldest friends gave them the cold shoulder. But I didn't. I just took hold of her hand and silently walked home beside her.

"You all get your teeth brushed and get into bed," Mama said that night. "You got to get up early to go to work with me in the morning."

John and I snapped our heads to look up at her. "You ain't got no job," John said.

"I do now," Mama said, pulling the covers up to his neck. "I'm working at the store."

John whooped into the air. We loved going to

Henry's store. "This is the most exciting thing that's ever happened!"

It seemed that nothing exciting ever really happened in Morgan Hill and sometimes that could be downright disappointing but now things were looking up. We had no idea that in the next few months there would be things happening in Morgan Hill that would change our lives forever.

Chapter
TWO

-

We did the same things every morning at our house: Before light, Mama got up and lit the stove in the kitchen (if it needed wood we brought that in the night before) as I went to the well and drew some water. First I poured some into the water reservoir in the stove; then I filled up the wash-basin so we could wash our faces and hands. John usually tried to bypass the washing part. "John, ain't you got enough gumption to wash the matters out of your eyes?" Mama asked each day.

"My face ain't dirty," he would say. "All I did

last night was sleep." But he would lose that argument.

John went to the chicken coop and gathered up the morning eggs, and then we both fed the pigs and went to the barn to milk the cows. The Pet Milk Company out of Greeneville came through Morgan Hill and bought milk from people just like us. Between the milk we sold to them and the chickens and eggs we sold to Henry, we were able to buy, as Mama said, "anything we couldn't grow or kill ourselves." At one time we had as many as nine cows but in time Daddy sold five of them to pay off gambling debts. He tried to sell our kitchen table and chairs, too, but those belonged to Mama's parents and she threw a royal Southern fit. She got the beating of her life that night but when morning came, the table and chairs was still there.

I didn't mind seeing the cows go; my hands got sore and cramped pulling and squeezing on their udders twice a day, and I tired of Flo lifting her great hoof and placing it squarely in my bucket. I despised milking with John because every morning he'd aim a teat at me and squirt a long stream of milk into my face. During the war he'd yell, "Bomb the Japs! Bomb the enemy," and then blast me.

We always poured our milk into a big five-gallon bucket and lowered it into the well. The milk stayed cooler there than in our icebox. At one time Daddy said, "Fran, that bucket of milk's goin' to spill and spoil that well water." Mama never let him lower it down or draw it up from that day on because she knew that if *anybody* was going to spill it, it would be him.

"What you put in your well always comes up in your bucket," Mama would say to him. It was years later when I realized that she wasn't really talking to him about wells or buckets.

Daddy used to skim our milk through so he could sell the cream but Mama put a stop to that. "Youngins need the whole milk," she said, squaring off to him one day.

We didn't make much money selling milk and eggs but it was something. My mother wasn't frugal; we didn't have enough money to be frugal. She was able to make do on next to no money at all. One winter during hog-killing time she made sousemeat (the hog's ears, feet, and other parts that were boiled down and formed into a loaf). Even Daddy couldn't eat it when he was good and drunk. I think the hogs thought twice about it before they ate it.

After breakfast we started the two-mile walk down the railroad track to the store. We walked the tracks instead of the road because they provided a straight shot right into town. Our farmhouse was set up along a bank so we'd walk down stairs Mama's own daddy had cut into the ground onto the tracks.

From the tracks we could see the back porch of Beef Hankins's house. Since Beef lived so close it had made Daddy's all-night poker games real convenient for stumbling home afterward. Beef's wife, Ruby, sat on the back porch staring. She was always there when we passed. During the school year, if we timed it just right, John and I could get ahead of Beef and Ruby's little girl, Louise. She was as homely as Beef and from what I'd seen in school just as dumb. We never wanted to walk with her because of "her no-account daddy."

John let his overall straps down. "Lord, I'm gonna die out here in this heat." The heat of the rails could leave our feet blistered so we walked beside the tracks, the honeysuckle hanging low off the bank and filling the air with one of the unmistakable smells I would later associate with that spring and summer.

"Winter will be here soon enough, John," Mama said. "Then everything will die off because of the cold."

"I ain't wantin' it to be cold. I just ain't wantin' it to be so daggum hot."

"You have to go through the heat of the summer and the dead of winter. Everybody does."

Mama looked up and waved at Ruby—Ruby didn't wave back.

"Why you reckon Miss Ruby never waves back?" I asked.

"Because she's quiet," Mama said. It seemed to me that sometimes people were quiet by nature. People like Joe Cannon. But other times it seemed they'd been made to be quiet—that something, or somebody, had sucked the noise right out of them. If a voice could be chained, Ruby's was.

"She can't wave cause bats laid eggs on her head and they bore down into her brain and she's gone crazy," John said. "That's why she stares all the time."

"Bats don't lay eggs on your head," I said.

"They lay eggs on your head and they squish down into your brain and eat it plum away. Then you go stark raving mad."

"Hush up, John," Mama said. "It's too early in the morning to be talking about bat eggs and brains. Bats don't do that, no how." But I walked the rest of the way to the store that morning with my hands folded over my head, just in case.

There was something magical about spending time in Henry's store. It had, like all country stores, a distinct smell—a blend of a wood-burning stove, pepper, bologna, and bins full of coffee, fresh milled flour, dried beans, potatoes, cabbage, tomatoes, and seeds of all kind. A Coke machine sat at the entrance of the store full of ice-cold bottles of Coke, Dr Pepper, and Orange Crush, or "orange Dope" as we all called it. Shelves lined the store walls and they were loaded with bread, canned vegetables, and milk, washing powder, peanut butter, and saltines. Sacks of chicken, cattle, and horse feed sat piled in the middle of the store and on the front porch. Old men like Gabbie Doakes (who, in his words, had "made peace with work years ago") would hurry down to the store in the morning to loaf, which meant sitting around and doing nothing. They'd loaf for hours, laughing, trouble swapping, and chewing tobacco, spitting into a brown-crusted can they'd carry with them. Henry always kept a pot of coffee brewing on the stove for customers. The counter was covered with big glass containers that were filled with licorice whips, malted milk balls, chocolate nonpareils, and other candy, and at the front of the store by the window sat a long refrigerated unit filled with several five-gallon containers of ice cream on one side and bologna, cheese, ham, and eggs on the other side. Henry kept a washtub by the counter filled with Moon Pies, Sugar Daddys, Baby Ruth, Milky Way, and PayDay candy bars. It was a child's paradise.

Besides the school building, Henry's was the first place in Morgan Hill wired to electricity in 1944. Half the community showed up to stare at the single lightbulb hanging from the ceiling. We knew electricity was in big cities but never imagined it would ever come to our little community in the middle of nowhere.

Whenever we went to the store, John and I would fall over each other to turn on the radio so we could listen to Maxine Harrison read the countywide news. The news was broadcast first thing in the morning and then the extended news, complete with obituaries, was read at noon. In a pinched, strained voice Maxine read the death announcements. "George Cass of Mosheim died last night at his home," she'd say without a trace of inflection. "He was eighty-nine. Cause of death is unknown."

"Unknown?" Loretta said. "Good Lord, he was eighty-nine!"

When my daddy died days earlier John and I had run to the store when we knew it would be announced. Maxine read two obituaries before my father's: a baby that was stillborn and somebody's father who didn't even live in Tennessee anymore but somewhere in Indiana. "Don't ya think that if they say your name on the radio that you should at least be dead here in the county?"

John asked. I hushed him when I heard Daddy's name.

"Charles Lonnie Gable died Thursday in Morgan Hill," Maxine had droned, her monotone voice sounding particularly bored that morning. "He was twenty-eight years old. Cause of death was problems from diabetes. He is survived by a wife and two children." Then Maxine moved on to the next obituary.

I stared at the radio. "She didn't say my name!" This was my one opportunity to hear my name on the radio and it was gone.

"She didn't say mine neither," John had said.

"She sure did yammer on and on about them other survivors of dead people, but when she got to us she just blowed right over our names," I had said, throwing my hands in the air. "How many times do you get the chance for your daddy to die?"

When we walked into the store the morning Mama started work, Henry clapped his hands together. "I'll be going into Greeneville this afternoon to buy more horse and chicken feed. Who wants to come with me?"

Whenever the opportunity came up to go out of town Mama would never let us go, always saying the same thing: "They'll hit you over the head with something." I'd never heard Maxine

Harrison read any obituaries about people dying after being hit over the head in Greeneville or Morristown but Mama said it happened. I always wondered what people were being hit over the head with: Was it a baseball bat or some sort of big caveman-type club? We could never take the train anywhere, either. "They'll hit you over the head and then trample you to death," she'd say.

"Can we go, Mama?" I asked.

"No. They'll hit you over the head with something." I don't know why I even bothered to ask.

Henry asked Loretta to help load the truck with groceries but she was quick to point out that her back was out. "Oh, that's right," Henry said. "Come on, Jane. Help me box up these groceries for your mama."

Part of what Henry did, or rather what he took upon himself to do, was to deliver food and anything else they might need to the old folks in Morgan Hill. If they were unable to pay for what Henry brought them he left the packages anyway. He and Loretta were not well off, they struggled like the rest of us, but if somebody was hungry Henry made sure they at least had a loaf of bread and a jar of peanut butter to get them through the night.

I grabbed a box and put it in the back of Henry's truck. "Henry? Is Loretta really down in her back?"

"Yep."

I stared up at him, thinking. "How long you reckon she'll be feeling puny?"

He stopped and lifted my face toward him. "Don't know. Why?"

"Well, I been thinking that maybe she's not down . . ."

"Sometimes we can think too much," Henry said. "And if we think too much then we might be inclined to know too much and sometimes ignorance is bliss." I was confused but nodded in agreement.

We put sacks of flour and sugar and boxes of canned goods in the back of the truck and watched as Mama shoved the truck into first gear and lunged out onto the road.

Fran's last delivery of the day was to the Cannon farm. She pulled into the driveway and saw Joe's mother, Helen, fussing over little Rose who was crying, touching a bright red wound on her forehead. "What happened?" Fran said above the wailing.

"She fell off the back of the truck," Addy said.

"She's got no business out on the farm," Helen

said, squeezing the little girl to her. "Do you, Miss Violet?"

"I'm not a violet," Rose said, whimpering.

"That's right, Miss Petunia."

"I ain't no petunia, neither. I Rose."

She poked Rose's belly with her finger and the little girl squealed. "That's right, Miss Rose." Fran carried the box of goods toward the door. "Leave that right there, Fran," Helen said. "That goes to Addy's house."

Addy stepped toward the box. "That's not ours . . ."

Helen didn't let her finish. "Who wants some pie?" Rose jumped to the floor and raced toward the door. "Adelia, I'm taking Rose in for some pie and then I'm laying her down for a while. You can come get her when you finish up for the day." Addy craned her neck to see where Rose was inside.

"She lost a son to a farming accident years ago," Fran said. Addy stared at the door. "It's all right." Fran seemed to know that Addy was worried about having her child, a black child, inside a white home. "Helen Cannon loves youngins."

Fran opened the truck door. "Jump in. I'll drive you down to your place." Addy held the box on her lap as Fran ground the gears into place and lunged down the gravel road that ran behind the Cannons' barn. The old clapboard house was made up of one room with a smaller room used for storing canned goods and vegetables off the kitchen. A small pallet made up of blankets lay on the floor.

Fran handed things to Addy out of the box. "You born and raised in Mississippi?"

"I was born in Alabama, but we moved all over from one farm to the next. My mama and daddy are dead. The rest of my family's scattered. I met Willie Dean in Mississippi."

Fran noticed a small locket around Addy's neck. "That sure is pretty." Addy opened the plain locket and revealed a tiny picture of her and Willie Dean on one side and Rose and Milo on the other.

The box was empty. Fran picked it up and glanced out to the truck. She turned back to Addy. "Addy . . . not everybody in Morgan Hill is like what you saw yesterday."

Addy smiled softly. "I know that. It was just some. It's always just some." Fran headed to the truck. The spring on the screen door clanged as she pushed it open. "Thank you, Miz Gable."

"Call me Fran." She looked at Addy and thought she should say something else but the words never came. She walked to the truck, putting a hand on her stomach.

"How far along are you, Miz Fran?" Fran's

face dropped. "A woman who's with child always puts a hand over her belly when the sickness comes over her, just like you did right then. You didn't know you did it. The sickness makes you do it. I know. It comes and goes. Does anybody know yet?"

"Henry and Loretta."

"Your youngins don't know?"

Fran sat on the porch and shook her head. "No, I've been waiting." She looked down at the ground and put her hands on the back of her neck, shaking her head back and forth.

Addy watched her. "You ain't hoping you'll lose it?"

"A hundred other things could be worse."

Addy stared out into the grove of pine trees that stood in front of her home. They were quiet, listening to the sound of the afternoon train blow its way through Morgan Hill. "I started picking cotton when I was four years old," she said.

Fran couldn't imagine Addy working in the fields. Her face was as pure as little Rose's and her hair was kept tidy, braided and twisted up behind her head. Her small frame didn't seem suited to work in the fields but her hands were marred from the work.

"I hated them hot mornings when the sun baked down on me and the sweat soaked through my dress and I hated it when them dry, prickly hulls would make my fingers crack and bleed." Addy rubbed her hands together, tracing the marks left from those early years in the fields. "When we loaded up on the wagons each morning I could see the white youngins running around and playing up at the big house, and there were so many days when I'd just stand in the middle of that cotton and cry because I wanted to play, too. But Mama always told me that colored youngins don't play until the cotton is picked. Every now and then the wind would carry the sound of them white youngins laughing and carrying on and it made my heart as sore as could be.

"One morning when I was around twelve I'd had enough. I said, 'Mama, how much mo' cotton am I gonna has to pick?' She said, 'I don't know, but I do knows that you's supposed to pick it . . . for now.' I said, 'Mama, I'm tired.' And she hollered out, 'Of course you's tired. We's all tired! But you ain't got no choice. You didn't pick this race . . . you was *chosen* for it, and there ain't nobody said it was gonna be easy. They'll be times when you'll be hot and tired and nearly dead, and nobody will even offer you a cup of cold water . . . but some will, and they'll offer just enough to keep you's runnin'. They won't be a lot of peoples along the way, but they'll be some and yo Mama will always be one of them.' "

Addy paused and smiled. "I love hot mornings now because they always remind me of my mama." Fran looked into the grove of pine trees. "Miz Fran, I don't know nothing about the race you're running. All I know is that if you want I'll be one of them people who'll give you a cup of cold water."

Fran looked down at the dust covering her shoes and clacked her feet together. "I might need a great, big pitcher of water."

"Then I'll just keep my well full." Addy leaned on her knees. "One day you'll look back and wonder how you ever made it through—how you ever got to the other side . . . but you did. We always do."

There are a few rare times in life when you feel you've found a friend for eternity. Fran felt it that day. She got up to leave. "You come on down to the store any time," she said.

Addy stood and looked at Fran's belly. "Don't you worry about that one, Miz Fran. He'll fight and kick his way into the world if he has to."

"Why do you think the baby's a he?"

Addy smiled. "My mama said that boys bring on more sickness early on when you carry them.

You need to give him a strong name. A name that will get him through."

Fran put her hand on her belly and knew that the baby would need more than a strong name to get him through but she didn't say that to Addy. She smiled but wished what Addy said was wrong, that the baby wouldn't fight its way into the world. She wished it wouldn't come into the world at all.

Pete Fletcher stopped by the store and put a nickel in the Coke machine on the front porch, pulling out a Dr Pepper. Henry handed John and me a nickel, too. "You two have been working all day. Get yourselves a dope and sit down here with me and Pete." I opened the door of the Coke machine and pulled out an Orange Crush.

Pete jumped to his feet and walked to his truck. "John, I've got something for you. I found this the other day and thought you might like to have it. My brother brought it back with him from the war." He handed John a pilot's cap complete with long earflaps and goggles.

"Holy cow," John said. "I've always wanted one of these." He put the cap on and the earflaps hung well below his chin. He pulled the goggles over his eyes and smiled. "How do I look?"

"Like a bug," I said.

"Like a genuine fighter pilot," Henry said.

John ran out and buzzed around the gas pump. "Take that, you dirty rat," he shouted, making firing noises.

I sat next to Henry on the swing and groaned when I saw Beef, Dewey Schaeffer, and the rest of the boys, Clyde Frank and Martin Lands, pull up. Beef, Clyde, and Martin worked together but Dewey wasn't from Morgan Hill. We rarely saw him. He worked at a lumber mill ten miles away. Dewey had dark wavy hair and blue eyes that matched the sky. Women thought he was easy to look at but even at my age I sensed there was something untamed about him; maybe that's why women found him good looking. I don't know. They were the same group of men who'd been with Daddy the night he died. Sometimes they'd play cards at our house but Mama would always take John and me somewhere else. "Sure would be nice if you stayed, Fran," Dewey always said. Mama would hold tight to our hands and pull us outside before any of the boys could talk to us.

"Afternoon, Jeff," Henry said. Nobody called Beef "Jeff." Nobody but Henry. Beef was a barrel-chested man with a thick neck and a round, swollen face. Regardless of the time of day, sharp, black whiskers spread across his cheeks and neck like dark moss. His hair was kept shaved close to his head. For the rest of my life I would associate the name Jeff with someone big, fat, and lazy. I once asked Henry why he called Beef "Jeff" and he said because it was his name. Beef fit him better. Henry said he knew Beef from the time he was just a little-bitty boy (I couldn't imagine Beef being a little-bitty anything). He said his daddy was worthless and that his mama had run off, leaving Beef to raise himself.

Beef nodded. "Henry. Pete." He didn't say anything to John or me. He never did.

"You boys grab a CoCola and join us," Henry said. I squirmed. Who would ever want Beef and the boys to join them?

"You all working today?" Pete asked, tipping the end of the Dr Pepper to his mouth.

"We're thinkin' about it," Dewey said, shoving a pinch of snuff between his cheek and gums. He howled out a raggedy laugh produced from too many cigarettes. "Course we don't want to think about it too much cause then we might actually get a mind to do it." Pete and Henry laughed along with Beef and the boys. I wondered if they were laughing like that the night my daddy died.

"What job are you all working on?" Henry asked, pushing the swing back and forth with his leg.

"Clyde and me supposed to head over Johnson City way for a school they're buildin'," Beef said, wiping sweat from his forehead. "But we never cottoned too much to goin' to school the first time 'round so we ain't in too much of a hurry to get there this time, either." The boys cackled at his stupid joke.

"But you'll get paid for it this time," Henry said.

"That ain't a good enough reason," Clyde said, rousing more laughter from Beef and Dewey. Clyde was a thin, wiry man. His small face was pockmarked and his brown hair was always greasy and flat to his head.

"You all heard about them niggers in town?" Beef asked. I stopped breathing. John stopped buzzing around the gas pump. Was he calling the Turners niggers? Did he think little Rose was a nigger?

"What're you talking about, Jeff?" Henry said.

Beef took out a can of tobacco and tapped it into a cigarette paper, rolling it with his fat, puffy fingers. "Them niggers that showed up at church on Sunday."

"Everybody's talking about 'em," Clyde said, slipping his greasy hands into his overall pockets. "Said they marched right up to the front and sat down."

"You must have seen 'em, Pete," Beef said, picking tobacco off the end of his tongue. "Word is you introduced 'em." Pete leaned forward in his chair. I don't think John had taken a breath since Beef first spoke the word "nigger." Beef puffed on the end of his cigarette. "I always thought niggers had their own churches."

Pete took a long drink from his Dr Pepper. "I didn't know that. Did you, Henry? Beef, where does it say in the Bible that colored people have their own churches?" I could see a vein on Beef's sweaty forehead begin to bulge. He'd come to gossip but Pete was making him look foolish.

"Some niggers tried that over Pulaski way and they lynched 'em," Beef said. "Strung 'em up and taught the rest of 'em a lesson." My heart beat faster. I'd heard Henry and some of the men talk about lynchings before but they always seemed worlds away from Morgan Hill. I pressed in close to Henry's side.

Henry wrapped his arm around me. "Jeff, you and the boys been coming around here for years and I don't mind your company but you need to clean up your talk today." Henry's voice had changed.

Beef looked at Henry and glanced at me. I held my breath. Beef shrugged and smiled. "All I'm saying is some folks don't like them *people* going to church with us." He blew out a puff of smoke.

Pete stood up and leaned against the door.

"With us? You mean with people like you and me? Because that's where you're confusing me, Beef. See, I haven't seen you at that church in fifteen years or more." Beef didn't flinch. Neither did Pete. Here was a man who could barely stand and talk in front of the congregation, yet now he was standing up and holding his own with Beef and the boys.

Henry set down his Coke. "Jeff, the Turners are working here. They're raising their family here. They're good folks. They ain't hurting nobody. Now why don't you and the boys sit down here and have a Coke with us?"

The cigarette hung out of Beef's mouth and smoke swirled up, melting his eyes into wrinkled slits. "No thanks, Henry," he said, climbing back into the truck with Dewey, Clyde, and Martin. "We need to get on." He pulled away and Pete and Henry watched the truck disappear around a bend in the road.

Pete took off his cap and sat down, rubbing his head. We watched the dust settle on the road and nobody said a word. "I don't think I'm cut out for any of this."

"Somebody's got to be cut out for it, Pete," Henry said. "Cause the Turners ain't going nowhere."

We all sat together in the silence. A truck

pulled up for gas and John made a beeline for the pump handle. Pete slapped Henry's back. He didn't say good-bye; he just got in his truck and pulled away, still rubbing his head. I stayed quiet on the swing, pulling both my knees up under my chin.

"Why you reckon everybody hates the Turners?"

Henry crossed a leg over his knee. "Hate's an awfully powerful word, Pretty Girl."

"Then why do you think nobody *likes* them?"

He paused, pulled his ankle up on his leg, and sighed. He knew there was no way I was going to drop this. "Afraid, I guess," he said, rolling the Coke bottle back and forth between his hands. "But it's not everybody, Jane."

I lifted my head and looked at him. "But it's an awful lot of them. Are they afraid cause Willie Dean's so big?"

"No, I reckon they're afraid because it's strange to have a colored family living right here in Morgan Hill." I kept looking at him. "Ain't nobody really used to that and, since things have been the same around here for so long, it's a hard thing for some people to get used to."

"But the Turners ain't gonna change anything."

"But some people think that if the Turners live

here then all sorts of colored people will move here and turn Morgan Hill upside down."

"But they just want some place to live," I said, resting my chin on top of my knees. "Seems that makes 'em like us."

He put his hand on the back of my neck and sighed. I put my head back down on my knees. It was easier to think that way. Henry swayed the swing back and forth. We both watched John clean the windows of the car at the pump, his earflaps bouncing up and down with every stroke across the windshield.

"Henry, why did Beef and the boys call them niggers?"

"Don't pay Jeff any attention, Pretty Girl. He's all talk. He always has been. As far as I know Jeff Hankins ain't ever struck a soul in this community but he sure does love to run that mouth. He'll talk to Ruby like she is a dog. If he wasn't stirring up trouble he wouldn't know what to do with himself. But he's just like the rest of us otherwise." I looked up at him. There was no way in this world that Beef was like us. "He's got a great big puddle of tears beside him that nobody can see."

"You think the Turners will come back to church?"

"Don't know. We'll see."

Henry squeezed my shoulder. "Beef won't do a thing, Pretty Girl. Don't worry about that. And folks will come around. Just give 'em time." But for once I didn't know if I believed that what Henry said was true. I wasn't so sure of anything anymore.

On our walk home Mama noticed the pilot's cap on John's head. "That thing will make your head sweat and give you the fits," she said. I sighed. It seemed life in Morgan Hill was crumbling around me and now I had one more thing to worry about.

I helped Mama clean up after supper. She was washing a skillet when she reached for a towel and held it to her mouth. She tripped over a chair and flung the screen door open, running into the yard.

John and I ran behind her and watched as she threw up in the grass. "What's wrong, Mama?" John yelled, running toward her. "Are you sick?" He always had a gift for asking or stating the obvious.

She straightened up and walked back to the house. "I'm having a baby," she said.

John and I stood with our mouths open. How could she have a baby when she didn't have a husband? Neither one of us knew how babies were made and we weren't about to start asking questions now. Like all good Southerners learn at an early age, we didn't ask any questions. The less we knew the better.

On a sweltering Sunday afternoon in July the Turners, Cannons, and Henry and Loretta came for a visit. Joe and Willie Dean threw horseshoes while Del Cannon sat in a cane-back chair and whittled sticks—he didn't make anything out of them, he just whittled them down to pointy, little nubs. Rose stuck each creation in her pocket as if she were hiding gold. Helen, Addy, and Mama cooked together inside the kitchen and we could hear them laugh till they cried. Even Mama. "Lord have mercy," we heard her snort. "Good Lord in Heaven!" We'd heard her laugh more in the last three months than we had in years. There were times I think she forgot she was pregnant. Before dinner we kids headed to the creek with Henry.

Addy stood next to Fran on the porch and watched the kids run down the embankment. "I'm so tired I could fall over right here," Addy said.

"Well if you do, fall that way and not on top of me. I might not be able to get back up." Everyone had noticed that Fran's belly was expanding. She looked at Addy's neck. "Where's your locket?"

Addy shook her head. "I don't know. I reckon it fell off a day or two ago. I've been everywhere looking for it." She touched her neck where the necklace used to hang. "How's that baby?"

Fran stared off toward the barn. "It don't move that much."

Addy reached over and put her hand on Fran's belly. "Hello, child."

"What are you doing?"

"You never put your hand on your belly so I thought I better." Fran didn't look at her. Addy cocked her head and smiled. "You can ignore me all you want, Fran Gable, and pretend that that baby ain't in there but that don't make it so. That baby is growing and these big dresses you're wearing prove it."

Fran leaned against a post on the porch. "Who asked you to come over anyway?"

"Somebody said I could come over any time I wanted."

"Well, that somebody was crazy."

Addy slapped her leg. "I'm gonna say a prayer that that baby ain't as ornery as his mama."

Fran put her hand on her belly. "The baby just kicked me."

Addy threw her hands in the air. "He's heard you out here fussing and is taking up with me." She placed her hands on Fran's belly. "What a fighter he is."

Fran pushed Addy's hand away. "This baby's kicking because you're going on like some sort of crazy fool."

Addy watched her and smiled. "I can go on home if you want. I could even go all the way back to Mississippi. That'd be a shame though because we sure do like it in Morgan Hill."

Fran sat on the porch step. "Well, you might as well stay now that you're here."

Addy sat next to her. "And why's that? Is it because you'd miss me if I was gone?" Fran didn't answer. "Would you miss your friend Addy Turner if she didn't live just down yonder?"

Fran didn't look at her. "Well, I ain't got a whole lot of friends so you might as well be one of them."

Addy leaned in to her. "Well, I'd miss you, too, you stubborn fool. I thought Willie Dean was the most stubborn person I'd ever met but I believe you got him beat." Addy bumped Fran with her shoulder and Fran lost her balance. Fran straightened up and brushed Addy with her shoulder. They bumped each other till they both ended up on the ground.

"I'll say this," Fran said, brushing off her dress. "It ain't been a bit boring since you turned up in Morgan Hill."

Addy threw her head back and laughed.

I can't recall how long we stayed at the creek and listened to Henry's stories, but I remember the laughter and the deep feeling of happiness I had on that afternoon. Maybe it's our way of wanting to remember things—gloss over the bad and replace it with the good—but it never works out that way. Not in real life. In real life you have to take both. There's no way around it. I remember wishing that summer would never end, that school would never start, and that winter would never come. But it would. Winter would come for all of us.

Chapter
THREE

That night Helen Cannon tossed in her bed; something was pulling her out of sleep. In the distance she thought she heard something—it sounded like a dog. She listened for a moment but couldn't hear anything more so she fell back to sleep; but there it was again, louder this time and closer to her ear. She opened her eyes and realized a dog was barking right outside her window, a gasping bark that lifted her out of bed. She stumbled into the hall and opened Joe's bedroom door. "Joe, I think Fred Dog's got an animal trapped outside the house."

Joe threw off the blankets and pushed open the screen door of the porch. "Oh my Lord," he screamed.

I don't know if it was the car lights in the window that woke me or if it was Doc Langley shouting as he ran in the door.

"Fran, get up! They need you at the Turner place."

I bolted upright and jumped out of bed to the window on John's side of the room. I could see Mama in the darkness running to Doc's truck. I ran for my overalls and screamed at John. "Wake up!"

"What?" he asked, then fell back to sleep.

I ran and shook him. "Something's going on. Something's happened." I shoved his overalls in his hands and dragged him out the door. We ran through the backfields that would take us to the Cannon farm and stopped when our sides hurt.

John doubled over. "I can't run no m-m-more, Jane." I grabbed him by the hand and yanked him toward me.

"Come on," I shouted. I felt sick to my stomach. Why would Doc wake Mama up in the middle of the night? Was Addy sick? Did something happen to little Rose? My heart raced faster as I led John through the rows of tobacco. Then we saw it. Great big orange flames licking high into the air. We ran toward them.

As we got closer, I saw Del and Joe Cannon and other men dragging water from the well to pour on the flames. People were screaming and yelling and running all around us. Where was Mama? Where were Milo and Rose? I ran right in the middle of the commotion and saw Henry dragging Mama away from the house. She was kicking and screaming. "Oh, God! No! No, God! No!"

I screamed for her. "Mama!"

Henry spun on his heels and saw us. "Somebody get them youngins out of here!"

Loretta was closest to us. I don't know how she did it but she ran toward John and me and grabbed each of us under an arm and carried us to Henry's truck. "Mama!" we both yelled, crying. "Mama!" Loretta started the truck and sped away. John and I turned around and pressed our hands against the back window. Tears streamed down our faces as we watched the flames reach higher and higher into the night.

Loretta took us to the Cannon house where we could make out part of the flames above the trees.

We stood at the window and she pulled us close. "Your mama's all right," she said over and over. We wrapped our arms around her and cried, frightened at the thought of what could be happening.

An hour passed, maybe ten for all I knew, before Doc ran into the house carrying Milo. Henry, Helen Cannon, and Mama were right behind him along with Nona Dodd and three other women.

"Put him there in that room," Helen said.

We ran into the room and I could make out Milo's body through the small spaces left between the adults. He was wearing underpants. Doc threw open his bag and yanked out his stethoscope and other things I couldn't see. I pressed hard, wedging myself between the grown-ups. John crammed himself in next to me. Part of Milo's legs had bright pink patches on them. Doc jumped up from his side. "His lungs are good and his burns aren't bad," he said, running from the room. Loretta and Nona scrambled around Milo's side, pressing cold rags onto his skin. Nona blotted his face and neck with a cold cloth. I have no memory of what they said in that room—all I remember is how tenderly they touched Milo and how they soothed and comforted him when he couldn't even hear them.

I heard yelling at the front door. John and I ran into the hall and saw Joe coming through the front door carrying Addy. Mama was right behind him. I looked around them expecting to see the men who would be carrying Willie Dean and Rose.

Helen pointed to her bed. "Here, Joe." He laid Addy down and adults flew all around her.

"I need water, Helen," Doc said. "And bring me some sheets or something to rip up." Helen and Joe left the room and Mama crumpled on a chair next to the bed. "Fran, find me some scissors." Mama jumped from her seat and Doc grabbed needles and bottles out of his bag. I walked up to the bed. Addy's skin had large, pink patches in some places but there weren't many burns. Her hair was singed, breaking off onto the pillowcase. I stepped closer; her face had scarcely been burned. It was still beautiful. Her body began to tremble and shake. I watched her, feeling myself go cold with fright, and reached out to touch her.

"Get back, Jane," Doc said, making me jump. John pulled me to him and we held hands. Doc drew medicine out of a bottle and injected it into Addy's arm. She was unconscious but screamed in pain—a frightening, horrifying scream that sent shivers down my spine. Helen, Joe, and

Mama all ran back into the room, throwing Doc his supplies. Henry picked me up and moved me and John to the corner as the home filled with more people scurrying around Addy's and Milo's beds. I can't name everyone who was there that night but I can still hear the whispered prayers. *God help them. God save them.* Time moved far too slow in that room. Much too slow. Mama sat next to Addy's bed and caressed a part of her hand that hadn't been burned. After working on Addy for what seemed like hours Doc stood to his feet. He looked at Henry and Loretta, then to Del and Helen and Joe Cannon. Mama looked up at him.

"There's nothing I can do." His words hung over the room like a thick mist and stung as I breathed. I must have misunderstood him. He was supposed to say, *Her burns aren't bad.* Just like he had for Milo.

"Give her something," Mama said. "Give her something to . . ."

"I can't help her. Her lungs are too far gone. All I can do is ease her pain." Tears flowed down Helen Cannon's face. "She has some time. Maybe a couple of hours. I don't know."

Mama began to sob; the tears that never came for my father flowed for Addy. "Oh, God!" she moaned, stroking Addy's hand. "Oh God, oh God, oh God. What's happened?" Joe hung his head and slid down the wall to the floor. Helen sat with her head in her hands and Del knelt down beside her. Loretta cried at the foot of the bed. John wrapped his arms around Henry and I stood holding on to Henry's hand, praying that I'd wake up.

I looked out the front door, watching Fred Dog run back and forth in front of the porch. Where were the men carrying Rose? Where were the ones who were helping Willie Dean into the house? Henry put his hand on my shoulder and I pressed my head against the screen door. "Where are the men who have Rose?" But in my heart I knew. I knew men were standing helplessly by letting the fire burn out before they could reach her body. I knew they were shaking their heads and watching the flames, wishing they could have done more to save Willie Dean and his baby girl. But they couldn't . . . and I knew it.

They found Willie Dean and Rose together near the front door. Willie Dean was on top of her, his arms wrapped around her. From what I've been told six men removed their bodies from the house, never once saying a word to one another. One man pulled a tarpaulin from the back of his truck, laid Rose back in her father's arms, and covered them with it. That's all I heard and all I could ever bear to know.

I walked back into Addy's room and saw everyone waiting just as before. Loretta was holding John tight in her lap. Mama was still by Addy's bed; her face was red but she was no longer crying. Addy's breathing came in wheezing gasps. Doc stood with his fist clenched over his mouth. Even though he had watched other people leave this world, I don't think he'd seen a death as painful. Helen kept dabbing a cold cloth to Addy's forehead, hoping in some small way that that would ease her pain. We didn't talk. We just stood by and waited.

"Fran." The voice was small. We all snapped our heads to listen. "Fran."

Mama leaned closer to Addy, her eyes once again wet with tears. "What is it, Addy?"

"Where's my babies?"

She couldn't tell her that Rose and Willie Dean were dead. She stroked Addy's hair. "Milo's fine. He's in the other room and he's going to be okay."

"Where's Willie Dean and Rose?" She was looking at Mama. A single tear fell down Mama's face. She shook her head and looked away. I wrapped my arms around Henry and squeezed tighter.

"I tried to get to them. But I couldn't."

Mama leaned forward in her chair and tears streamed down her cheeks. She rested her head next to Addy's. "Shh, shh, shh."

"Fran," Addy said. "Fran." Mama raised her head. "Would you take care of my boy?" Her words were steady.

Mama nodded. "Doc and I will take real good care of him."

She tried to move her hand toward my mother. "No. Would you bring him into your home?" Tears fell off Mama's chin. "Would you raise him, Fran? You're still young. You got youngins his age. We ain't got nobody else. Would you help him?"

"Yes," Mama said. "Yes, I will." She patted Addy's forehead with the cold cloth and looked in her face. "I will, Addy. I will." She said it over and over until Addy closed her eyes.

I heard Helen's cries first. She sat down beside the bed and covered her mouth, the white skin pulled tight over veins that spread out fine and blue in her hand. Giant tears streamed down the old woman's face. Loretta picked John up and left the room. I felt Henry moving me toward the door but I stood firm, staring at Addy's body. I wanted her to move. I kept staring, willing her to breathe again.

"How did this happen?"

The question broke the silence and startled me. It was a question we'd all thought about but pushed out of our heads. Nobody said anything. Mama asked it again, still touching Addy's face. "How did this happen?"

"Fran," Henry said.

"Did somebody set that fire?" Her voice was rising. "Somebody answer me." Nobody moved. Nobody knew what to say. She flew off the chair. "Did somebody set that fire, Henry?" Her eyes blazed and I shrank back. She ran for the door. Joe grabbed her by the arms and stopped her. "Was that fire set, Joe?" she sobbed, sliding through his arms. "Was it set?"

"We don't know, Fran," he said, holding on to her. "We don't know."

John and I sat together in a chair watching Milo sleep, making sure that he didn't die. John fell asleep and his head wobbled around on my shoulder before hanging off the side of the chair. Henry slipped into the room and stood by the bed. "Will Milo die, too?" I asked, watching Milo's chest move up and down.

He pulled the sheet over Milo's arms. "Doc said he'll be fine. He didn't get enough smoke in his lungs." Henry put a pillow on the floor and laid John down, covering him with a blanket. He squeezed my leg and I got up so he could sit down. I crawled onto his lap and hung on to his neck, so afraid that somehow I would lose him.

I nestled my head beneath his chin. "Are you going to die, Henry?"

"I don't plan on it anytime soon."

"How'd Milo get out?"

"Joe broke out a window and got to him and Addy."

"You mean he jumped right into the fire?"

"The flames had just reached the room where Milo was sleeping. Joe busted out the window, grabbed him, and handed him out to Del before running into the rest of the house."

I stayed quiet, thinking about what Henry said. I remember Joe carrying Addy into the house but he didn't look like he'd just come out of a burning house; he looked the same to me as he did that first Sunday he got back from the war. He didn't look like somebody who'd fought a war. He just looked like Joe. "Did Rose know she was dying?"

"I don't think she did." I wanted to believe him. I wanted to believe that the smoke filled her lungs before she ever felt a flame hit her body.

"But Willie Dean did, didn't he? They found him on top of Rose so he had to know."

"Willie Dean jumped up and did what he needed to do. All he thought about was his family."

"Can they see us now?" I tried to picture Willie Dean, Addy, and Rose in heaven but all I could think of was Addy's dead body and the image of Rose and Willie Dean.

"Well, since there's no sadness in heaven I suspect they're not looking down here—cause if they did they'd be awfully sad right now."

I thought about that a long time. "Where was God when that fire was burning? Why didn't he put it out, Henry?"

He rested his head against the back of the chair. "I don't know. All I know is there's a whole lot of things that we'll never understand." I wondered if Willie Dean and Addy understood everything now. I wondered if they knew why they all died and Milo didn't.

Mama came in and stood at the foot of the bed. She looked drained. Her eyes were small and red.

"Is he going to be living with us?" I asked.

She nodded. I watched her stare at Milo and

wondered how in the world we could all live together—how Milo would ever live without his own family and how people would treat my mother, a widowed white woman, for letting a colored boy live in her house. I thought and thought and thought about those things until I drifted off to sleep. Henry laid me on the floor next to John and covered me with a quilt.

Mama pulled up a chair and sat next to Milo's bed. She sat there until he woke up, and then she told him. She told him everything.

I didn't run to Henry's store the next day to hear Maxine read the obituaries. I didn't want to think that while she was reading about the fire that broke out on the Cannon farm that people were just carrying on with their lives as if nothing ever happened, although I knew there were farms to farm and cows to milk and gardens to weed. Life would go on without the Turners.

Henry, Pete, Del, and other men worked throughout the morning to haul off what was left of the Turner home. "Milo don't need to be reminded of what happened every time he looks out at this," Henry said to me, throwing blackened boards onto his truck. I stepped through the warm, charred rubble, pushing singed boards to the side with my foot, looking for anything that would remind Milo of his family. "There's nothing here," Henry said, resting his hand on my shoulder. "Nothing's left, Pretty Girl."

After Helen got a few bites of biscuits and milk into Milo, I watched as Joe carried him to his truck. I moved another board with my foot. "Your mama needs you, Jane," Henry said. I shook my head. I didn't want to go home, not after what happened, not now with Milo there. Henry lifted my chin to look at him. "Your mama's gonna need you at home, Pretty Girl. Get on now."

I picked up Fred Dog and held him in my lap in the back of the truck. He needed a place to live, too.

It was a Tuesday morning when we buried Willie Dean, Addy, and Rose. The cemetery was full; many of the people who had disliked the Turners' presence in our church came out that day to mourn for them. Several pickup trucks pulled into the church filled with black people I'd never seen before. They made their way to the cemetery and surrounded Milo. "Who are they?" I asked Henry.

"They probably heard Maxine on the radio and have come from Greeneville."

"Why?"

"To pay their respects, Jane."

I looked around the cemetery and saw my father's gravestone for the first time since we buried him—*Charles Lonnie Gable, Feb 3, 1919–May 20, 1947.*

"These stones sure don't say much, do they, Henry?"

"It's all right there in the dash," Henry said, pointing to the dash between the year of birth and death. I looked at the line. "That's a person's whole life, Jane. It all comes down to how you live out that dash."

"But nobody knows what happened by looking at that little line."

"The people who matter know."

"I'll always know," I whispered to the top of the Turners' caskets. *"I'll always remember."*

Pete opened his Bible and read from the book of Isaiah. "Fear not," he said, reading. "For I have redeemed thee, I have called thee by thy name; thou art mine. When thou passest through the waters, I will be with thee; and through the rivers, they shall not overflow thee: when thou walkest through the fire, thou shalt not be burned; neither shall the flame kindle upon thee." Amens rose from the black people among us. I looked up at their faces. Why were they agreeing with what Pete read when flames had

79

killed the Turners? Pete kept reading. "Behold, I will do a new thing; now it shall spring forth; shall ye not know it? I will even make a way in the wilderness, and rivers in the desert."

A low hum rumbled around the graves followed by *"Yessir! Uh-huh! Amen!"*

I glanced from one black face to another. Many of their eyes were closed but as if with one voice they sang "Amazing Grace" as the men of our church took hold of the grave straps and started lowering the caskets. I dug my fingers into Henry's leg. He picked me up and I buried my face in his shoulder. I couldn't watch the men do that this time. Tears streamed down Mama's face, but she kept her hand clenched over her lips as if she'd burst if a sob or a moan came out. Helen Cannon crumpled Milo into her side, holding tight to him, but Milo didn't cry. He watched the caskets disappear into the ground and never made a sound.

Chapter
FOUR

For the second time in less than two weeks people converged on our home, laying out a massive spread of food over the back of wagons and this time leaving clothes as well—a pair of overalls, shirt, or shoes for Milo. Even the people who never welcomed Willie Dean and Addy to our community left something for him. They'd smile, unsure of what to say to an orphaned black boy but hoping their acts of service would make up for any prior coldness toward his family. John and I stayed out on the porch again, this time

with Milo. We sat in silence as we nibbled at our
food, giving most of it to Fred. Mama walked
through the yard and stopped in front of us.
"Did you eat?" We nodded and she walked away.
John and I tried to act normal around Milo, but
nothing was normal and everybody knew it.
There was a colored boy living in our home—
nothing would be normal again.

Helen and Del walked onto the porch. Helen
sat down next to Milo and wrapped her arms
around him. "We loved your mama and daddy,"
she said, tears rimming her eyes. "And we loved
little Rose." She pulled Milo closer to her. "There
are good, decent people in this world, Milo, and
your mama and daddy were some of the best."
She laid his head on her shoulder and patted his
arm. Where others couldn't find anything to say,
Helen said very little, but it made all the differ-
ence in the world. She took hold of Milo's hand
and sat with him the rest of the afternoon.

Fran shuffled between people in the yard and
wished that most of them would go away. *How
long are you going to let him live with you, Fran?*
someone asked. *You could probably find a colored family right away who would take him in,*
someone else offered. She found herself surrounded by four women offering, in their words,

a way out of this mess and advice on *what they would do,* when she felt Margaret's hand on her arm. They escaped to the back porch and sat down on the steps.

"How you doing, Fran?"

"I'm fine. Tired."

Margaret nibbled on a piece of coconut pie. "Is there anything I can do?"

"No. I don't know. I can't think right now."

Margaret leaned in close. "People are saying that you're taking that boy in."

"That's right."

"You're actually going to raise him?"

"I'm going to try."

"How are you going to manage that?"

Fran shook her head. "I don't know but I promised his mama."

"You can't do that, Fran. It'd be too much on you."

"I've made it this far. Surely I can take on one more."

"But that boy ain't no relation."

Fran looked out over the railroad tracks. "I promised his mama."

"That don't matter. You ain't able to do this. How you gonna take him on and the baby you're carrying?"

"I don't know."

"You don't have to do this, Fran." Margaret leaned further in, whispering. "He's a colored person."

Fran felt the pressure in her head swell. She rubbed her temples and stood to her feet, tired to the bone. "We're *all* colored people, Margaret." She walked away before Margaret could say anything else. She made her way toward the kitchen door but stopped when Joe caught her attention.

"You look like you need to sit down." As he led her to the wagon where Loretta had left a steaming pot of coffee she could see the cuts and burns he received in the fire on his arms. He handed Fran a cup. "That'll put hair on your chest. Loretta made it." It was a known fact that Loretta could make anything but a good cup of coffee.

She took a sip and swallowed hard. "That's some of the worst coffee I've ever had."

Joe picked up another cup. "Since misery loves company." They walked to the side of the house and sat under a maple tree Fran's father had planted. "Listen, Fran. The men have been talking. There's no way to tell if the fire was started."

"I know. I knew it that night."

Joe ran his finger through the grass. "I think they left a lamp burning and it caught on a curtain or a blanket." Joe hung his head. "It'd be easier to think that somebody set it. That way there'd be somebody to blame."

Fran braced her back against the tree and looked up through the branches. "I keep thinking we're all just gonna wake up." She squinted as the sun hit her eyes. "I remember when I was little and Preacher Hale talked about Lazarus being raised from the dead. He said, 'Mary and Martha wanted Jesus to heal their brother, but God basically said, that's your way, but I've got a better way.' There's been a lot of times in my life when I've wondered about that better way. I'm having a real hard time seeing what that better way is right now." She shook her head. "I can barely raise my own youngins, let alone . . ."

"Fran," Joe said.

"I can't raise him, Joe."

"Yes, you can."

"I don't know his ways . . . his people's ways. I don't know nothing about being colored or raising a colored boy. He'll never accept me as his mama."

Joe set his cup on the ground. "That's *all right,* Fran. You're not his mother. He'll remember and love his own mama. Addy had to know that her boy would have a home."

She lowered her head. "But every time I look at him I know I can't do it."

"Addy knew you could. That's why she hung

on as long as she did, so she could ask you to take care of her boy." She looked up at him and a tear fell down her cheek. "She knew you could do this, Fran." She wanted to tell Joe that he was wrong, that she couldn't do it because she was scared and unable to make ends meet, but she didn't. She just nodded and brushed the tear away.

When everyone left I helped Mama put food into the icebox. We took a sack of potatoes and onions to the cellar, and as Mama lowered the clapboard door we heard a squeal. The squeal grew louder and Mama ran to the side of the house to see Milo at the edge of the pasture throwing rocks at Fred Dog. "Go on! Get out of here, you stupid dog," he said, chucking another rock that hit Fred's backside. The dog yelped and ran into the pasture and stopped. "Go on!" Milo screamed, throwing another rock that hit Fred's chest. "I hate you!" Fred ran farther into the pasture but stopped to watch Milo as Mama ran to Milo's side.

"Milo," she said. "Stop throwing rocks at Fred."

"I hate him," he said, heaving a large rock toward Fred. "He ain't my friend no more." He leaned down to pick up another rock.

Mama took it from Milo's hand and knelt in

front of him. "Fred *is* your friend. That's why he's standing right there just waiting for you to stop throwing rocks at him because he wants to come over here and be with you."

Milo hurled another rock toward Fred but missed. Mama grabbed his hand. "Hurting Fred ain't gonna bring your mama and daddy back. He's sad, too, you know." Milo picked up another rock and chucked it as hard as he could into the pasture, away from Fred this time, and marched off. Fred followed him into the barn where they both stayed till evening.

Milo wouldn't eat any supper and Mama didn't force him to, but she did make him come inside to go to bed. He stood by the bedroom door as John crawled into my bed with me. "Do you need to run make water before you lay down?" she asked. He shook his head and ran out onto the porch. John and I jumped out of bed to see him through the window.

Mama opened the screen door and it slapped behind her. She found Milo holding on to a post. John and I pressed our ears up to the window screen to hear. "It's late, Milo. Come on into bed. You need to get some sleep."

"It ain't fit for me to sleep in there. I'll sleep here."

Mama sighed and sat on one of our cane-back

chairs. "The porch is where Fred Dog sleeps. People sleep in yonder in the beds."

He shook his head. "It ain't fittin' and I know it."

She stood and put a hand on his shoulder, turning him so he could see her. "People in this house sleep in beds."

"But it ain't . . ."

"People in this house sleep in beds." She stood behind him and guided him toward the door, but he kept a hand on the porch railing. "Well, hold on a minute and let me get my pillow and covers."

"What for?"

"I can't let you sleep out here alone." She opened the door leading into the kitchen.

"You can't sleep out here."

"Why not?"

"It ain't right."

"It ain't right for you, either, but since you're gung ho to do it, then I'm going to sleep out here with you. Course if you wanted to sleep in your bed then I'd sleep in mine, and we could figure out another night to come sleep out here."

Milo thought for a moment and nodded. John and I scrambled back into my bed and watched as Milo crawled into John's bed. Mama pulled the covers up over each one of us. She didn't kiss us; it wasn't her way. She said good night and closed the door behind her. Then in the quiet we heard Milo turn toward the window and I knew he was crying. He had done the same thing the night before. We turned our heads and looked at his back. We didn't know what to do so we listened as he cried himself to sleep.

I don't know if Mama ever fell asleep that night. Her face was drawn the next morning and the dark patches under her eyes were a deep purplish gray. "Come on," she said, walking into our room. "You all get up." She walked over to Milo's bed and looked at him. "You want some breakfast, Milo?" He didn't answer. "Come on. Get washed up."

The sound of Mama slurping her coffee, John gulping his milk, and forks scraping our plates was the only noise that broke the silence at the table. "You need to eat, Milo," Mama said. I looked up and noticed he hadn't taken a bite of anything. He stared down at his plate.

"Them sausages are real good," John said. I shot him a look that told him to shut up.

"Milo, you need to eat," Mama said again. "You ain't had anything since yesterday afternoon." Milo looked at his plate. We sat in the quiet and the ticking of the mantel clock in the front room sounded like a bomb ready to go off.

A minute went by, or maybe ten, but it felt like an hour with that deafening tick-tock drumming in our ears. Mama stood and took the plate from Milo. "I'll wrap it up. You might want it later. Jane, you and John show Milo what to do. You all need to get out there and start milking them cows before the milk company gets here. We don't want to be late for the store." I looked up at her; we weren't supposed to go to the store today. Henry told Mama to stay home. "Go on, Jane. Don't make me tell you again."

If it weren't for the milk hitting the bucket or the occasional moo from a grumpy cow, there wouldn't have been any sound in the barn, either. We poured the milk into the cans and finished twisting on the last lid when the milk truck pulled up the driveway.

Mama took the money and walked to the house while I put our milking stools away. I heard thumping on the side of the barn and peeked around the side to see Milo hurling rocks. He threw one after the other. I left him alone and went to find Mama.

She was in the backyard lifting the clump of earth she kept on top of the hole she'd dug for the coffee can. She put the few dollar bills inside and shoved the can back into the hole.

"Mama, you don't got to do that no more," I

said. She turned her head to see me standing behind her. "Daddy's dead. You don't have to hide the money no more." She wiped her hands on her dress and looked back into the hole, nodding.

"Milo's throwing rocks again."

"At who?"

"Nobody. He's throwing them at the barn."

"Leave him be then." She pulled the coffee can to her chest and walked to the house. "You all finish up. We need to get to the store." I fetched the bucket of eggs we'd sell to Henry and looked for Milo. John was pitching hay from the barn loft to the stalls below.

"Milo with you?" He shook his head. I looked through each stall and in the grain bin before running around the barn. Where was he? I ran around the house and then looked both ways on the railroad tracks before running to the kitchen; the screen door slammed shut behind me. Mama looked up from washing the dishes. "Milo in here?" Her look was confused and I ran through the house calling his name. She followed. "He ain't here," I said. "He's run off."

Sleep never came for Joe Cannon; each time he'd drift off he could hear Addy's cries from inside the Turner home. "Oh God, my babies," she said as Joe picked her up that night.

He arose early and carried a lamp to the barn. The cows picked up their heads and one by one stood to their feet, the barn awakening with the sounds of anxious cows ready to be milked. He looked forward to the work; it helped keep his mind off the fire.

Joe was a quiet man. In his letters home he never talked about what was happening to him in Europe. All his family ever really knew was that he was a rifleman, and since there was already another man named Joe in his unit, the men called him Cannon. After a man in his unit died it was Joe's duty to write every parent and spouse and spell out for them how their son or husband died and what, if any, were his last words. Joe was still writing those letters when he returned to Morgan Hill. Years later he was still getting letters of thanks in the mail but the memories were too hard to keep within reach so he put them away. Out of sight. Out of mind.

Somebody came up with the idea to write "our boys in the war" once a week, so each week somebody in Morgan Hill would write and tell of what was happening back home. Joe said it was the letters from home that kept him going and he saved every one of those.

Joe slapped the backside of the last cow he milked and her belly scraped the reddened skin on his arms. He grimaced and touched his fingers along the burns. He reached for the balm he used on the cows' udders and spread a thin layer over the wounds. Joe studied his arms and tears stung his eyes. In his mind he ran into the Turner house over and over again and had time to get them all out. Addy never screamed for her babies because they were already safe outside the house waiting for her.

"You been up all night?" Joe jumped at his father's voice, rubbing his face along a shoulder to dry it.

"Pretty much. Milkin's done."

Del watched as Joe tightened the lid on the last milk can. "Your mama has breakfast ready. Why don't you go on in the house and eat and then get some sleep?"

Joe kept his back to his father. "I'm all right, Pop. I'll be in in a while."

"You ain't needing to stay here, Joe," Del said. "You need to get back to Atlanta. Me and your mama will be all right."

"I'll stay on till I can find somebody else to come help."

"But that might take months. You need to go on back to your work."

Joe pressed the base of his hands into his eyes and rubbed hard. He reached for a hoe hanging on the wall and made his way to the tobacco patch. "We can chew on it later, Pop." With Willie Dean and Addy helping on the farm, Joe and Del had decided to set out two acres of tobacco, an acre more than they were accustomed to planting. Joe looked out over the rows of tobacco and wondered how his father could tend to two acres on his own. He knew Del was right; it would take months to find someone else to come help on the farm and he needed to get back to Atlanta.

Joe stabbed at the ground with the blade of the hoe and dug up a small patch of weeds growing between two plants. He stopped when he thought he heard something. He began working again but stood still when he heard another distinct sound. He remained quiet and rolled down his shirtsleeves to cover his burns. He looked out over the patch and walked toward the sound. At the back of the patch, near the grove of pine trees, he saw two little bare feet. He crept closer and saw Milo lying on the ground, his arm covering his face. Joe leaned on top of the hoe.

"Milo?" Milo flinched but kept his arm across his face. "What are you doing?"

"Just laying here waiting for my daddy and mama to get to work."

That tore at Joe's heart and he sat on the

ground next to Milo. "Does Fran know you're here?" Milo shook his head. "Well, you've probably got them worried to death down at the Gable place."

"I ain't gonna stay there no more."

"Why not?"

"Cause I live with my mama and daddy and Rose."

Joe took his handkerchief out of his pocket and rubbed the back of his neck. "They ain't here no more, Milo."

Milo slid his arm over his head and looked at him. "They'll be back, Mister Joe."

Joe's mind reeled back to the war when shots blasted close to his head. He always hoped the worst hadn't happened and that his brother next to him would get up and walk away but it never happened. Death isn't that gracious. "They can't come back." He placed his hand on top of Milo's head and felt his throat thicken. "They can never come back."

Milo rested his forehead on his knees and rocked back and forth. "They gotta come back so we can live together and Mama can make supper." Tears filled his eyes and Milo buried his face between his knees. Joe put his arm around Milo's shoulders and pulled him close. "They left me alone here. They gotta come back to get me."

"Your mama asked Fran to take care of you."

Milo shook his head back and forth on top of his knees. "Them people are white."

"They're good . . ."

Milo stopped him. "Coloreds don't live with white people."

Joe nodded and looked into the sky. "I guess we ain't seen it around here. You're right. But if that's written down in a rule book somewhere I sure don't know about it." He put his hand on the back of Milo's neck and squeezed. "Your mama would have given anything to stay here with you, Milo. And as long as I live I'll believe that she held on as long as she did to make sure she knew that you were taken care of." Milo looked at him. "She wasn't about to leave this world until she knew that you were safe and had a home to grow up in."

"But they's white."

"Guess your mama didn't notice that."

Milo lay back on the ground, slung his arm over his face, and thought about that for a long time.

Chapter
FIVE

Joe drove Milo back to our house that morning. Milo stood on the porch and dug his toe between two boards. "I'm sorry, ma'am," he said.

Mama pulled him into her and rubbed the back of his neck. "You ain't got a thing to be sorry about."

Milo didn't say a word as we walked down the tracks that morning to Henry's and our words were just as few. The silences were long and painful. Fortunately the sun got hotter and the heat hurried our steps.

"That little nigger boy livin' with you now?"

The words rang out in the stillness and a shiver ran down my spine. We all looked up the embankment and saw Beef and Clyde smiling at us from Beef's porch. Mama took hold of Milo's hand and threw up her other hand in a wave. "Mornin'." She appeared to hope that if she left Beef and Clyde alone they'd leave us alone.

"I don't think Lonnie'd be too happy knowing what's going on at his house," Clyde said. Mama held tighter to Milo's hand and I grabbed John's, pulling him along. "He wouldn't like that nigger smelling up the place."

I felt my heart in my throat and ran to keep up with Mama.

"He's a pretty little nigger," Beef yelled after us.

Mama paid no attention. She walked on and drew Milo closer to her side. "Boy, this heat's something, ain't it?" she said, trying to get Milo's mind off Beef and Clyde. "I want to know who put the order in for all this heat."

"Me, too," I said, trying my best to distract Milo. "It sure is hot."

Milo kept his eyes on the tracks and swung the tin pail Mama had packed with biscuits and sausage. "My daddy says I ain't supposed to listen to people like that."

"Your daddy's right," Mama said. "I know you can hear them but don't you ever listen to them."

A boy named Alvin Dodson often hid behind the honeysuckle bushes alongside the tracks waiting for John and me to pass. I don't believe there was a boy on the face of the earth that I hated more than Alvin Dodson. When school started in the fall he was going to be in the fifth grade for the second time and was twice as big as the other kids. He had a mean streak that started in his big toe and shot out the top of his head.

Each morning on our way to school Alvin jumped out from behind the bushes and mashed a fist full of cockleburs into my hair till it was a knotted mess. Then he'd push John down and run away. (He had tried to rub the cockleburs into John's hair, too, but since his hair was always so short to his head they never stuck.) By the time I made it to school John and I usually had all the cockleburs out, along with massive chunks of my hair. Some day I hoped to settle the score.

"But, Jane," Henry had said. "You might be the only glimpse of kindness that Alvin ever sees on some days. How will it look if you act just as mean and nasty as he does?" I'd think about

what Henry said about kindness later after I had
taken my full revenge on Alvin.

Alvin was waiting for John and me that morning but he hadn't expected to see Mama or Milo
with us. I couldn't see him behind the bushes but
I knew he had to be there. Mama did, too.
"Morning, Alvin," she said, staring ahead of her
on the tracks. We heard a rustle and saw Alvin
peer at us from behind the bush.

"That colored boy livin' with you?"

The anger I felt toward Beef and Clyde rose to
my throat. "You just keep your snotty nose out
of our business, Alvin Dodson! This ain't your
business no how so just get on out of here."

"Jane," Mama said, scolding me. "All he did
was ask a question."

"That snake's questions ain't fit to answer," I
said, loud enough for Alvin to hear.

"I'll give you what for someday," Alvin said,
picking at the bush.

I stopped and turned around, screaming. "I'll
give you what for if you rub one more cocklebur
in my hair, you dumb hick!"

Mama took my arm and hurried me down the
tracks. "What is wrong with you? You are just
eat up with meanness this morning." I watched
Alvin run up the embankment and plotted how I
could get back at him one day.

◆ ◆ ◆

Henry kept Milo close to him at the store, teaching him how to run the cash register and what to do behind the counter, but every time someone came in that morning, they'd shoot Milo a quick well-practiced smile but then look at their shoes or rub an imaginary spot on their sleeve to avoid eye contact with him. Many came to talk about what happened, to get to the bottom of the fire and, when Mama wasn't in sight and they didn't think John or I could hear, question my mother's sanity for taking a colored boy into her home, but it was too hard to talk with his little black face looking back at them.

A horn sounded and Henry and John stepped toward the door to fill a car up with gas. "You're in charge till I get back," he said, whispering to Milo. When the tank was full Henry stepped back inside, peering over the counter. "Where's Milo?"

I looked up from my sweeping and Mama stepped away from a shelf she was stocking. "He was right there," she said.

Mama and I looked through the aisles and Henry walked to the back of the store and opened the door of the stockroom. He motioned for Mama that he'd found Milo and stepped inside the room, sitting down beside him. "I didn't want to run the cash register no more," Milo said.

"I've been thinking," Henry said. "I need to line up all these canned goods in neat, straight rows but I just don't have time to do it. I don't know how I'll get it done."

"I could do it."

"Well, I hadn't thought of that. But you don't want to do that. You'd have to be back here in this old, dusty stockroom all day."

"I don't mind."

Henry rubbed the back of Milo's head. "Okay then. Let me show you what to do." They stood and Henry pointed to the first shelf. "Keep everything in its own group. Like here's the salmon. Line the cans up three in a row starting at the back." He moved the cans around. "There. Now they're real easy to count. Think you can do it?" Milo nodded and Henry lifted his face, looking at him. "You come on out any time you want." Henry closed the door behind him.

Mama, John, and I flocked Henry at the counter. "What's going on?" Mama asked.

He raised his hands. "He's fine, Fran. He's going to straighten up the stockroom for us."

"Straighten what up? There's nothing to . . ."

Henry stopped her. "He needs to be left alone,

Fran. He doesn't want to be out here with everybody looking at him. Let's just leave him be."

By late morning Milo still hadn't opened the door of the stockroom. "He's fine," Henry kept saying. "He'll come out when he's ready."

John and I didn't try to beat each other to the phone when it rang that day. We didn't do anything at all. "There's nothing as deafening as grief," Loretta said. "No matter what you do it just rings loud in your ears."

Dinnertime rolled around and Milo still hadn't opened the door. Mama knocked and held a bologna sandwich and glass of milk out to him. "Are you hungry?" He shook his head, and continued working on a row of lima beans. "I'll leave it here then." She set the sandwich and milk on a shelf and looked at the rows of canned goods. "You sure are doing a good job back here. Henry's going to be so proud." Milo kept working without turning to her. "Well, it's right here if you get hungry."

Mama leaned onto the counter. "He's still not eating."

"He'll eat when he's hungry," Henry said, ushering John and me out the door to fill Olive Harper's car with gas.

Mama grabbed a rag and scrubbed at a spot

on top of the counter. Loretta took the rag from her. "He'll be okay, Fran. He needs to grieve in the way that fits him."

"I don't know what to say to him. I look at him and can't think of one thing to say to this little boy who has lost everything. What kind of person does that make me?"

"Makes you human, Fran."

I pumped the gas into Olive's tank while John washed her front window. Olive commented to Henry about the excellent help he was keeping and gave us each a penny before driving away. I ran up to the porch swing and sat down, stuffing the penny in my overalls pocket. "What if Milo don't come out? What if he stays back there forever?"

Henry sat next to me and laid his arm on the back of the swing. "He'll come out, Pretty Girl."

"What are we supposed to say to him when he does?"

"You don't need to say anything."

I took the penny out of my pocket and examined it. "Well, we'll be good at that cause there ain't nobody saying anything at our house."

Henry waved at a truck passing the store and I threw up my hand as well. "I loved my mother," Henry said, "but that woman never knew when to hush. You could ask her what time it was and she'd give you the history of the watch. Sometimes when I was a boy I wanted to say, 'Mama, don't say anything. Just sit down here with me.'"

I looked up at him. "I ain't got no idea what you're talking about."

He pulled me closer to him. "Sometimes it's just nice to be with somebody and not fill up every quiet space with a whole lot of talk." I leaned into Henry's chest and let every square inch of the porch fill up with quiet.

For as long as I could remember, once a week a man by the name of Hoby Kane drove the ice truck from Greeneville to Morgan Hill. In the South people were never called shy, they were called backward, and Hoby was as backward as they came. We didn't know what it was called then but Hoby had scoliosis of the spine. He was as crooked as anybody I'd ever seen but it didn't slow him down. He always carried lemon drops in his jacket pocket (he always wore a jacket to hide his spine) and I'd reach in and take one.

Despite our best efforts to lure Milo out with the excitement of Hoby's ice delivery he stayed in the stockroom all day. When Mama opened the door to tell him we were going home she noticed the uneaten bologna sandwich right where she left it but the glass of milk was gone.

Helen brought supper to us late that afternoon but Milo didn't eat. Mama jumped up and poured John and me a glass of milk. "You want some milk, Milo?" He nodded and Mama filled his glass to the top, setting the bottle beside him. She sat down and watched him empty his glass. Milo looked at the milk bottle. "It's all right," she said. "You can pour yourself another glass." He poured milk to the top and Mama finished eating, content that he was getting something in his belly. It was another hushed meal at our house. Mama didn't even make John take the pilot's cap off his head. We ate in silence and I prayed that I'd eat faster than I ever had so I could get up from the table and leave that misery as fast as possible.

We heard a truck pulling up our drive and I jumped to look out the kitchen window. "It's Margaret," I said with relief, grateful for anyone who would help stir up some conversation in our house.

Margaret crossed the porch. Fred barked but she leaned down and pet him and he burrowed his head into her leg for more. She peered inside the screen door and her face grew solemn when she saw Milo sitting at our table. "Knock, knock," she said, pulling the corners of her mouth up into a forced smile.

"Come on in," Mama said.

Normally, Margaret would grab a plate and nibble on whatever we were eating but today she stood at the door watching us. "Well, well," she said, fumbling for words. "I didn't mean to come at supper. I thought you'd be done."

Milo hung his head and Mama stood. "We are done," she said. "You all run out and play for a while." Margaret moved away from the door as John barreled past her. Milo never glanced up to see Margaret's eyes as he gently pushed the screen door open. I began to clear the plates from the table. "Go on, Jane. You can play, too." I ran out the door.

Margaret helped Fran clear the table. "You're looking tired, Fran."

"I am tired. Sit down there and I'll get you some iced tea."

Margaret watched as Fran poured the amber liquid into a glass. "How's he doing?" Margaret asked.

Fran scraped the remainder of food into a slop bucket. "Good as can be expected, I reckon."

"I heard about Beef and the boys today."

Fran stopped working. "Just ignorant talk."

"They'll make things hard on you, Fran."

Fran wrapped the corn bread in waxed paper.

"Beef and his friends ain't got nothing better to do than run their mouths. They've done it for years now. Everybody's used to it."

"It ain't just Beef and the boys, Fran."

Fran's face was somber as she turned. "What are you here to tell me, Margaret?"

"People don't think it's right that that colored boy is living here. You're a widow, Fran, and you ain't got . . ."

Fran leaned against the counter and put a hand over her mouth. "These people you're talking about do know that that little boy is an orphan, right?"

"Of course they do, Fran, but there are colored folks who would take him in. Colored people who know what it's like to raise a colored boy."

"His mama asked me to take care of him and I mean to do . . ."

"Only because she didn't know of any coloreds around here. If she knew there was some colored families close by, don't you think she'd at least want to consider them? That woman was dying. She didn't think she had any other choice." Fran turned to face the windows and watched the cows graze in the pasture. "Fran, it ain't right to be unequally yoked together."

She spun to look at her. "Are you quoting

scripture to me, Margaret? Because if you are you're sounding just as ignorant as Beef. Giving a colored boy a home ain't got nothing to do with being 'unequally yoked.' " Her face was flushed and her hands were shaking. "If you want to spout scripture to all them 'people' who're so upset that I have a colored boy in my home, you remind them of the verse that says that pure religion is to visit the fatherless and the widows in their affliction. It seems that there's both them categories in this home now. But the only people visiting us just want to stir up trouble."

"Fran, we been friends forever and you know I ain't meaning to make you mad." Fran turned back to her work and began dumping water from the stove into the washbasin. "I didn't come to stir up anything. I just wanted you to at least think about finding him a home with some colored folks."

Fran wouldn't turn to look at her. She scrubbed at the dishes so hard that water sloshed onto the floor. Margaret stayed for a few moments, hoping Fran would say something, but she didn't so she stood to her feet. "I just ain't wanting Beef or anybody else to hurt you, Fran."

The door closed and Fran hung her head. Her heart was pounding and her arms and legs were trembling. It felt as if her oldest friend was turning against her. She looked down at herself. Her dress was soaked through.

I checked under the bed for the bogeyman before John climbed in that evening. "All clear," I said.

"What kind of baby will Mama have?" John whispered.

"How am I supposed to know? Ain't nobody but God can know that."

"Where's the baby at?"

"Down in her belly."

"What's it doing in there?"

"It's getting bigger," I said, whispering loud. "Stop asking me so many dumb questions. I'm thinking."

" 'Bout what?"

I looked at him in the moonlight. "This baby ain't good news. It's another mouth to feed and you know as well as I do that Mama don't make enough money to feed all of us." John stared at me but didn't say anything. "We gotta find somebody who'll take all of us into their family."

"Who's gonna take all of us in with their family?"

"I've been studying on that since Daddy died but I ain't come up with nothing. I'll think of something though."

I lay awake staring at the ceiling for the longest time that night. I was already in a bind trying to find a place for the three of us to be a real family, but then when we added Milo to the mix it made the odds of finding a home for all of us go way down. He was one more mouth to feed and a colored mouth at that. Now with another baby coming, well, I couldn't even think about anybody wanting to take us into their family because there would be too many of us.

I could hear Mama in the kitchen arranging food in the icebox. John dug his elbow into my neck and I threw his arm off of me. I didn't know how he could sleep. I looked over at Milo but he was facing the wall. I threw the sheet off my legs and crept over to the door, opening it. I crossed through the front room and snuck into the hall that led to the kitchen. I could hear Mama moving but couldn't make out what she was doing. It was too quiet. I crept to the door leading into the kitchen and slid down the wall to the floor. I knew if she came out of the door she'd walk right past me. I pulled my knees to my chest and held my breath, waiting.

I lifted my head when I heard what sounded like a cat outside the house. The sound was distant and too soft to hear so I put my head back down on my knees. But there it was again. It was faint but I heard it. I raised my head and strained to hear the sound. I hated to think that an animal had the poor thing trapped. The sound came in waves this time and I crouched closer to the wall, not moving. It was my mother. She was crying. I turned my face toward the kitchen and rested one cheek on my knees, hugging them tighter to me. There sure was an awful lot of crying going on in our house, but nobody knew what to do about it.

I heard a chair scoot across the floor and I inched tighter to the wall but Mama didn't leave the kitchen. I edged closer to the door to see what she was doing and through the slats of the chair at the end of the table I could see her sitting, pressing her thumbs into her temples. Her bad ear was closest to the door so I stood to my feet, watching her. All my life my mother's strength made her seem so big to me but as I watched her I realized how small and slight she was. Throughout her marriage to my father she had often been left alone but I don't think she ever felt alone, not till now. I slipped back into the hall before she saw me and sat on the floor listening to her muffled sobs before I crept back into bed.

In order to give farmers time to cut tobacco and bail their fall hay the beginning of the school year always fell sometime after Labor Day. Although September was still weeks away Fran got up earlier than usual and walked past the store and up the hill that led to the schoolhouse. She hadn't told anyone she was going; she just took a notion to go that morning.

She caught her breath at the top of the hill before climbing the steps to the front doors. She swung them open and walked through the empty halls into Bill Jeffers's office. Bill had been the principal of the school for seventeen years; he handed Fran her diploma in 1937 and twice expelled Lonnie Gable for disorderly conduct. After his second expulsion Lonnie decided to give up on school altogether, figuring he had learned enough in ten years. Delores Cockburn, Bill's secretary for the last fifteen years, was at her desk. She was a sharp-faced woman whose thick brows made her look as if she had a permanent scowl. "Well, Fran Gable," she said. "What in the world are you doing here? School doesn't start for weeks."

"I know, Delores. But I need to enroll Milo Turner."

Delores looked over the top of her glasses. "I heard you took him in, Fran."

"That's right. I did. And I need to get him enrolled in school." Delores nervously pushed the glasses up on her nose and moved papers around on her desk. "What do I need to fill out, Delores?"

Delores moved more papers around and straightened her dress. "Fran." She coughed into her fist and straightened her dress again.

"I'll fill out the papers today, Delores."

Delores cleared her throat and looked at her. "I can't give you the papers, Fran."

"Why not?"

"You know we can't enroll a colored boy in school."

Fran felt her throat tighten. "Then where does he go?"

Delores was perspiring and her glasses began a slow slide down her nose. "He'll have to go into Greeneville, I guess."

"How am I supposed to get him to Greeneville? I don't have a car so how do I get him there?"

Delores pushed the glasses back up her nose. "Fran, I'm real sorry about his folks but this is a white school."

"He's living in my house!"

"But that doesn't make him any less colored. Now these aren't my rules, Fran. Coloreds attend their own schools."

"But there's never been any coloreds in Morgan Hill to start their own school. I'm talking about one little colored boy, Delores. He needs to go to school!"

Delores shook her head. "I'm sorry, Fran. I'm real sorry."

Fran walked to the door and spun back toward her. "This ain't right and you know it, Delores."

"I'm real sorry, Fran, but all I can do is follow the rules."

Fran yanked the door open and ran down the hall, straight into Bill Jeffers. "Well, morning, Fran," he said. "Where you going in such a hurry?"

"Fran would like to enroll the little colored boy in school," Delores said, her shoes clacking as she walked toward them. "I've already explained that we can't do that."

"Come on in here," Bill said, directing Fran to the office. She had great respect for Mr. Jeffers. He always treated each child with kindness. Bill's dark hair was graying now but he was still lean and mild tempered; a smile came easy for him. He closed the door so Delores couldn't hear and sat on the edge of his desk. "Go on and sit down, Fran."

"I don't want to sit. All I want is to enroll one little boy in school. That's it."

"Fran, I'm sorry about what happened."

"I am sick of people telling me how sorry they

are that that boy's parents are dead. Being sorry don't help me enroll him in school."

"I know what you're saying but my hands are tied here."

"Can't you see what this will do to that little boy? Can't you see what will happen to him if we don't help him? He's one little boy, Bill. One little boy who needs to go to school."

"I know that, Fran, but the state says there's not a place for him here."

She stared at him. "His parents are dead. I would hope to God that we'd do everything possible to *find* a place for him here."

"I know it doesn't make any sense, Fran. I think if you live in this community then you should be able to go to school here."

"Then do something, Bill."

He shook his head. "I can't."

"One day there's going to be more coloreds in Morgan Hill. You gonna keep pushing them out the door?"

"I'm not pushing them, Fran. I'm just doing what I'm told."

She stood and walked out the door.

The next day Fran got up in the half light of morning and lit the stove before heading to the chicken coop. She stopped when she saw a ragged piece of paper crammed into the coop's door. She unrolled it and her hands trembled as she read the words scratched across the page: *Get that nigger boy out of Morgan Hill before we do something about it.* Her heart throbbed in her throat and she shoved the note into her dress pocket, spinning in place to look around. She ran back inside the house and closed the door behind her, sliding into a chair at the kitchen table. Her hand began to shake and she grasped it, holding it tight with the other hand. A wave of nausea gripped her and she fled outside, vomiting by the well house.

Chapter
SIX

I walked into the kitchen to help Mama with breakfast. She poured buttermilk into a well she'd made in the middle of a bowl of flour. "Jane, I don't want you and the boys walking down the tracks for town anymore."

We'd been walking down those railroad tracks ever since I could remember. "Why not? Just because of Beef?"

"Just walk the boys down the road and don't argue with me."

"But the road's longer than . . ."

Her eyes blazed when she turned. "Don't argue with me, Jane. For once in your life just listen to me and stop arguing."

We walked down the road together. When we got to the store I noticed three customers standing near the cheese case whispering. They stopped talking when they saw Milo. I sensed Mama's body stiffen. We all knew they were talking about us. Without a word Milo disappeared into the stockroom again. I gave Henry a look. People sure weren't making it fun to be at the store anymore. Henry followed Milo and found him looking at the stockroom shelves. "I thought there was more to do," Milo said.

"There's a whole lot more to do but I didn't think you'd want to spend another day back here in this dark stockroom."

"I don't mind."

Henry looked around the room. "Well, you know what I've been needing to do back here? I need to paint all these shelves white. Now I know that means you'd have to take everything off the shelves and you just straightened them yesterday but we've been needing to paint these shelves forever."

Milo looked at the shelves. "I can do it."

"But it might take all day. Maybe even two days." Milo looked up at Henry but he didn't say a word. Henry smiled and patted his shoulder. "All right. Let me get the paint." Milo started emptying the shelves as Henry dug through the crates against the back wall looking for an old can of paint he'd stored there after he painted the porch a year ago. He pulled it out and walked to the front of the store for the screwdriver he kept under the cash register. He set the paint can on the counter and started to pry it open.

"What in the world are you doing back there today?" Loretta asked.

"Milo's going to paint the shelves and I imagine that means the floor will get painted in the process."

John and I never even knew painting was an option when we came to Henry's store and weren't about to miss out on it now.

Loretta rested a box of crackers on her hip and looked at Henry. "Who ever heard of painting a dingy old stockroom? What are you . . ."

Henry held up the paint can in front of her. "You'll need to excuse us, Missus Walker. We've got important work to do."

Canned goods were piled in the middle of the stockroom when Henry opened the door. "Okay, Pretty Girl. You're in charge of putting all these cans outside the door." I ran for the cans and shoved them down in my overalls and in my pockets and then dropped them outside the door. He poured paint into individual cans for us. "Here's three brushes. Stick your brush in the can halfway, pull it out, and scrape off one side like this. Then start painting." John and I couldn't wait to dip our brushes into that creamy white liquid. Henry looked at us and shook his head.

"What's wrong, Henry?" I asked.

"Your mama will tar and feather me if you get paint on them clothes. You better shimmy out of them and paint in your underpants."

John and Milo kicked off their overalls and I let mine drop, standing in my underpants and shirt. "Can I leave my shirt on, Henry? I get so cold when I paint." Henry laughed, gathered our overalls, and walked out the door. "Wait," I said. "Who's the boss?"

"I'm the boss," John said, poking his thumb into his chest.

"I'm the boss and you know it," I said.

Henry held up his hands. "Jane, why don't you be the foreman? John can be the overseer, and Milo can be the manager." We all thought about our positions for a moment and then smiled, each of us feeling that our individual title was the best.

When Henry closed the door behind him we

dipped our brushes into our cans till they were coated up to the handles and started slathering paint from one end of a shelf to the next. Midway through the morning John put his bucket of paint on a shelf closer to his work. "That ain't a good idea," I said.

"Hush up, Jane. You don't know a good idea when it bites you in the hind end."

Minutes later he stuck his brush in the can and pulled it down on top of him. I turned when he hollered, in time to see his face and chest covered with white. I fell to the floor laughing. Even Milo couldn't hold out. "Now you really are the whitest boy I've ever seen," he said. It was the first time since his family died that we'd seen a glimpse of the old Milo we had known.

By the time dinner rolled around we were coated with paint and had managed to get some on the shelves and walls. I stuck my head out the door when I heard Loretta calling us. "We need our britches to eat dinner," I said.

Loretta craned her neck to see us and turned away before laughing. "Henry Walker, what is wrong with you? Them youngins are naked!" Henry walked past her and peeked inside the stockroom. It looked as if the can of paint had exploded, most of it landing on John. The floor was covered with white footprints.

"What do you think, Henry?" I asked. Henry put his hand over his mouth and looked up and down the shelves, taking it all in. To his surprise the shelves that we could reach were mostly white. Paint dripped down the back of the wall behind each shelf and onto the floor below. "It's something back here, ain't it?"

"It's something all right," Henry said, taking our brushes before further damage could be done.

"We got a lot more work to do," John said.

"I can see that."

Milo took a few nibbles of a bologna sandwich before heading back to the stockroom. It wasn't much but the return of his appetite relieved Mama. We painted for the rest of the day. Looking back I know that stockroom was a mess. We had no business painting a fence post, let alone a room, and Loretta and Mama knew that. Thankfully, Henry didn't.

At the end of the day Henry helped us clean our brushes and we tried to scrub the paint off our hands and bodies. He walked behind the store and dug out a can of turpentine from the shed and soaked a rag with it before rubbing it into our skin. "Henry, we stink," I said, covering my nose.

Henry rubbed John's hands till they were dripping creamy, white liquid. "Well, you and John run out to the sink and wash this off before it dries. And don't pass any open flames on your way there."

Henry soaked the rag for Milo. "You all did some mighty fine work back here."

Milo looked around the room. "It's all done," he said. Henry rubbed the rag into Milo's arm and the paint loosened, leaving white flecks resting on his skin. "There ain't nothing else to do."

Henry looked at Milo and tears filled Milo's eyes. Henry squeezed his arm.

"I don't want to go back. I want to stay here," Milo said.

Henry wiped the turpentine across Milo's other arm. "You'd get terrible lonesome living in this stockroom." A tear fell down Milo's cheek. "And Fran, Jane, and John would miss you something fierce." He picked up a clean rag and dried Milo's arms.

"I don't want to go back." His voice was breaking and Henry stopped his work.

He sat on the floor next to him. "I don't blame you." Milo looked at Henry; he hadn't expected him to agree. "It's too much for a little boy to take in. It's too much for all of us." He rubbed his hand over Milo's head and pulled him into his chest. "It's awfully hard, ain't it?" Milo nodded. "But we always gotta get through the hard part before something is bearable." Milo looked at him.

"I've never told anybody this, but when I was a little boy I couldn't wait to grow up so I could move out of Morgan Hill. I heard stories about bigger towns that had cars and stores and even restaurants where you could go in and drink a cup of coffee at a counter and I knew that's where I wanted to be. Morgan Hill didn't have anything; it still doesn't, really. Not like those things, anyway. I'd walk along the railroad and look out on Widow's Mountain, which ain't a mountain at all but just part of the rolling hills back here. You know which one I mean? Looks like it's covered with soft, green moss?" Milo nodded. "I took a notion one summer morning that I wanted to climb that monster and I put some sausage biscuits in a sack and set off." He poured turpentine onto the rag and scrubbed Milo's feet. "It took me an hour or more to hike over there and when I got there I saw that the base of Widow's Mountain was nothing but a flat rock wall. It didn't look anything like the rest of the hills around here. Well, I stood there trying to figure a way up that rock and I walked back and forth and knew there was no way to get up it."

"What'd you do?"

Henry dried Milo's feet and rubbed at a blotch of paint on his neck. "I went home."

"You didn't get up it?"

"Nope. I went home and let another year go by, but every day I'd look at Widow's Mountain sitting over there so pretty and green and it got nagging me real bad. So one morning after I finished milking I set out again with a sack full of sausage biscuits."

"Did you get up it?"

He shook his head. "There just wasn't a way up that rock. So I turned around and went home again." He put the lid on the turpentine and set it off to the side. "But every morning there was that mountain hovering over me."

"Why didn't you go back?"

Henry smiled. "I did. A few months later I jumped out of bed before anybody else was up and I wrapped some leftover cornbread in a rag and I set off for that mountain for the last time. I was determined to get to that sweet grass on top. I marched around the base again and looked up that rock and noticed a space about this big where the mountain attached to the hill next to it. I was a scrawny boy and I figured that if I wedged my body in that crack that I could work my way through the crevice till I got a grip on the grassy ledge at the top of it. I started wriggling through there just like a caterpillar."

"Caterpillar's do like this," Milo said, inching his finger on top of his leg.

Henry nodded and rubbed the turpentine off his hands. "That's what I was doing. It was slow going but I finally made my way up that crevice and grabbed hold of the ledge that was jutting out, and I pulled and pulled till I shimmied my way out."

"Was it hard to climb up that mountain?"

Henry shook his head. "Nope. Climbing the mountain was easy. The hard part was getting through that crevice. That was the hardest thing I'd ever done. I was scratched up pretty good, both my elbows were bleeding, but it was easy street from that point on and boy did it feel good when I walked up that grassy hillside. When I got to the top I saw the prettiest sight on earth."

"What was it?"

"Morgan Hill. I looked out over the pastures and the tobacco fields and the gardens that were growing tall with corn, and I knew that I wanted to live here for the rest of my life. I sat up there and watched the train go by and the cows graze on the hillside and I knew I was home." Milo pulled on his overalls and Henry stood next to him. He lifted Milo's chin and smiled. "It sure would be nice if it could be your home, too." He helped Milo button down his overall straps. "Can you go back tonight?" Milo thought for a moment and then nodded, staring at the floor. Henry knelt down in front of him and whispered. "Fran Gable is one of the finest women I've ever known. She's good through and through. I believe your mama knew that." Milo fidgeted with the straps on his overalls, looking at the floor. "What's wrong, Milo?"

"I want to help with the tobacco my mama and daddy planted."

Henry smiled, held on to Milo's hand, and closed the door of the stockroom behind them.

If Milo was going to help with the tobacco on the Cannon farm, then John and I were going with him. When we walked up to the Cannons' the next morning, Joe and Del were already in the middle of the field working. "Milo's ready to come back to work," Mama said, calling out to them.

Joe pulled a handkerchief from his back pocket and walked toward us, wiping his face and neck. "It's hard work suckering them plants. You sure you want to do that?"

"We can do it," I said. "Me and John are gonna help."

Joe nodded. "Come on then." We followed Joe into the middle of the tobacco. "You all just find these little suckers like this and pinch 'em off before it stunts the growth of the plant. Watch Milo. He already knows how to do it." We reached for the small blooms and pinched them off wherever we saw them. It was a hot, miserable job suckering those plants in the middle of those tobacco rows but Milo never complained. I looked over at him throughout the morning and sweat glistened on top of his head and ran down his face. I ran my hand across my forehead and wiped the water onto my overalls.

"Lord, it's hot out here," John said.

I grabbed his arm and pulled him to me. "Don't say anything about the heat."

"Why not? It's hot."

"Just don't say everything so loud."

"But I'm about to die out here in this heat." He shook his head and went back to work.

Del and Joe didn't say much that morning. They weren't comfortable filling up space with talk that needed to be used for work but Joe seemed to know when we were getting weary. "You're doing real good work, Jane." He clapped his hand on my shoulder and squeezed it. "You all are doing real good work." I felt a surge of energy and ran to another plant. John beat me to it and together we pinched off every sucker we saw. I knew I wasn't working that tobacco just to help Milo; I wanted to help Joe, too. For some reason I knew Joe was what a man was supposed to be and I wanted to feel his hand on my shoulder again.

When Helen called us to the dinner table I scurried so I could sit next to Joe. He never let on like he noticed but when I sat down I felt his hand patting my back. "We got us the three best workers in the county," he said. I felt my chest puff up and realized what I'd missed in not having a father that was proud of me, one that made me feel like I was somebody. For the first time since my father died I felt sad and understood why Milo cried so much at night. His daddy wasn't there to clap him on the shoulder anymore.

At the end of July Milo helped Joe take the horse and wagon and tools back to the barn. "You going back to Atlanta, Mister Joe?"

Joe loosened the bridle. "Yeah, I'll be going back."

"When?"

"Soon as we get the tobacco in."

"You can't stay?"

Joe knelt down in front of him. "No." Milo's eyes were dark and lonely. "When I look in that barn I can still see your daddy sitting right over there milking the cows." He wiped his forehead with his handkerchief and caught the sweat running down his neck.

Milo squinted, looking into the barn. "I can't see him no more. I can't even see him when I close my eyes."

Joe's chest grew heavy; he lifted the bridle off the horse's neck. "You will. You'll see your daddy standing here by the barn hitching the horses or down by the creek pulling a great big carp out of the water. And you'll see your mama walking around with Rose on her hip or standing at the kitchen stove cooking supper." Milo put his hand on his forehead and squinted up at him. "When my brother Luddy died I was as sad as I could be because I couldn't see him anymore and I couldn't hear his voice, but one day I did. I walked through the house and I swear I could hear his laugh and I could picture him sitting at the supper table eating biscuits hand over fist." Milo dug his toes into the dirt. He didn't understand. "You'll see your mama and daddy in your mind," Joe said, putting his handkerchief back in his pocket. "And you'll always feel them." He felt his throat catch and put his hand on Milo's shoulder. "Let's go see what Mother has fixed for supper."

During the first week of August we had finished washing the supper dishes and were walking to the barn to do the evening milking when I saw Beef and the boys climbing the embankment to our house. "Mama," I whispered, pointing at them.

"Run on in the barn before they see you all," she said. "Take the boys up to the loft and stay there till I come for you."

"But, Mama—"

"Run now, Jane." I grabbed John and Milo by their hands and ran for the barn as Mama hurried to the house. She went inside the kitchen and grabbed a pot and sat on the porch beside a peck of beans she'd picked that morning, waiting for Beef.

"Wha, wha, what's g-going on?" John asked.

"Nothing," I said. "Mama just don't want us around for Beef's visit." Fred Dog saw the men and began to bark, leaning on his front legs and hiking his rear in the air. We ran to the loft and each found a knothole to peer through. I could just make out Mama on the porch when I saw Beef, Clyde, and Dewey walk up to her. Fred ran close to Mama and barked louder. She shushed him and made him lie down. If Beef laid a hand on my mother I intended to grab a shovel or pitchfork and knock it upside his head. I pressed my eye closer to the knothole.

"They're here because of me, ain't they?" Milo whispered.

"No," I said, lying. "Them are my daddy's no-account friends. My daddy was the most no-account of all of them and he owed them poker money."

Milo looked unsure but stuck his eye up to the slats of the barn wall, watching.

"Howdy, Fran," Beef said.

Mama picked up a bean and broke it into the pot. "Boys. What are you all up to today?"

"We haven't seen much of you since Lonnie died, Fraaan." Mama cringed. She always hated the way Dewey growled her name. "We knew he'd want us to check up on you."

"I'm doing good." She snapped more beans into the pot.

"Here," Dewey said. "Let me help you with those." He moved a chair in front of her and sat down with his leg rubbing against hers.

She shifted in her chair. "I can do it. There ain't many here. Thank you, though."

He moved closer still. "You work too hard,

Fran," Dewey said, inching his leg till it was pressed firmly against hers.

Beef looked around. "Where're Lonnie's youngins?"

"They're out running around."

"You let that little nigger boy run around with Lonnie's youngins just like that?" Clyde asked.

"Harmless play."

"Niggers ain't harmless, Fran," Beef said, leaning against a post on the porch. "People around here know that."

"Fran knows it, too. Don't you, Frannie?" Dewey said.

Mama's breathing grew shallow but her face remained calm. "He's a little boy, Dewey. He's as harmless as they come."

"Hell, Fran!" Beef said, spitting tobacco into the yard. "They ain't no nigger that's harmless. No wonder people are calling you a nigger lover."

Mama pulled the pot onto her lap and stood. Dewey got up and leaned against the porch rail. "I know you all are busy and I need to get these beans on to cook." I felt my breath catch when Beef moved in close to her face.

"Wha-what's h-h-he doing, Jane?" John asked.

"Shhh," I said. "I don't know."

"That little nigger ain't got no right in Lonnie's house," Beef said.

Mama put the pot on her hip and looked Beef in the eyes. "This ain't and never has been Lonnie's house. If it weren't for my daddy we wouldn't have a house at all."

Clyde and Dewey laughed. "Lonnie always said you were a spitfire, Fran," Dewey said, looking her over. "I bet he meant that more ways than one." She felt his eyes on her and slid back into her chair.

"Little nigger boy living with a widowed white woman," Clyde said. "Good God Almighty."

"You need to find that nigger a nigger home," Beef said. "That's the right thing to do. The good thing about Lonnie is he always knew the right thing to do."

Mama held the pot tighter to her. "No, the good thing about Lonnie is that he's dead."

Beef moved toward her but Dewey stepped in front of him and sat on his chair again, his knees straddling one of Mama's legs. She held her breath at his touch but looked him in the eyes. My heart pounded as I watched. "It ain't right for him to be here," Dewey whispered. "So you better find that boy a home." He moved his hand up her thigh as he stood to his feet. "Come on, boys. Fran's got them beans to put on."

I watched as Beef and Clyde walked toward the embankment and the tracks. Dewey ran his hand along Mama's arm and helped her up. She pulled it away and backed to the door. "You are a fine woman, Fran," he said, leaning close. "How in the world did Lonnie Gable ever get his hands on you?" She wasn't breathing but held his gaze. He flicked his cigarette butt onto the porch and walked away.

John ran for the stairs in the loft. "Not yet," I said, whispering loud to stop him. "Mama said to wait for her to come get us." I strained to see Beef and the boys walk down the embankment. I knew Mama would come for us only when she knew they were far away. I watched her on the porch but she wasn't moving. I wasn't even sure if she was breathing.

Days went by without another word from Beef or the boys. One morning John and Milo and I made our way to the barn to do the milking. We stopped when we saw Dandy lying on her side, her tongue hanging out of her mouth. A note was nailed to the barn wall. I ripped it down and read it before John or Milo could see that I had it. *We're getting tired*, it read. *Find that boy some place else to live.* I ran screaming for Mama.

Her mouth tightened as she read the note and

she scratched at red splotches on her neck. "W-w-what does it say, Mama?" John asked. She looked at Milo but didn't say anything. I wished John would keep quiet. "W-what does it say?"

Her lips formed a thin, trapped smile. "It ain't nothing but foolishness," she said, folding the note and putting it in her dress pocket.

"It says something, Mama!" John said.

"You all get ready to go to the Cannons'. I'll milk this morning."

"But, Mama," John said. He never knew when her nerves were stretched tight.

"Go now, John Charles, before I whoop your hind end!"

Mama knew we were all afraid so she walked with us to the Cannons'. "You all are early," Joe said, drinking coffee on the porch. "Fran, we didn't expect to see you this morning."

"One of our cows died," I said.

Joe stepped off the porch and looked at Mama. "How'd she die?"

Mama shook her head. "Who knows? Just one of them things." She walked back toward the tracks. "You all be good and work hard today."

Joe stopped her, looking down at her arms. "Those are hives, Fran," he whispered.

She ran her hand over her arm. "Heat rash. I get it every summer."

Joe handed his coffee cup to me. "Run on in the house and tell Pop I'll be back in a little bit."

"Maybe her heart gave out," Joe said, kneeling next to Dandy.

"Cows don't just die like that, Joe."

He ran his hand through his hair and shook his head. "I know." He bent close to Dandy's tongue. "We'll need to get Doctor Wilkes out here. I'll call him when I get back to the house. He'd know if she was poisoned."

"They killed her," Fran said, showing Joe the note. "Beef and the boys did this because *niggers* shouldn't be living in *Lonnie's* house." She slammed the stall door shut. "They're gonna come in here and kill off every single one of the cows we got left." Her voice was strained. "Then they're going to destroy my garden and burn down my house, just like they burned down the Turner house."

"Fran, they don't want Milo living here but them boys ain't murderers."

"What is that in there?" she asked, pointing toward the stall door. "You don't know what they'll do, Joe."

Joe remained quiet, studying the note. "I know

they'll scare a woman half to death by saying Lord knows what but this here ain't like Beef, Fran. To be honest he ain't smart enough to do something like this and he's too lazy. He wouldn't take time to sit down and write a note." He watched as she scratched her arms and leaned against the barn. "Fran, I'm going to go call Doctor Wilkes. Go on in the house and get some rest."

"I can't rest, Joe. I got . . ."

His voice was calm. "Go on, Fran. There's nothing you can do till Doc Wilkes gets here." She looked at him and tried to smile. Joe was so different from Lonnie. Lonnie would never have cared enough to insist that she rest.

People avoided real conversation with Fran at the store that afternoon. Word had spread about her cow and deep down everyone knew it happened because of Milo but each customer talked about the weather, pretending that was foremost on everyone's mind.

Fran sighed when Margaret came in for bread and sugar; although their previous talk hadn't gone well she was relieved to see her oldest friend.

Margaret laid her goods on the counter. "You're covered in hives."

Fran ran her hand over her arm and reached for the loaf of bread. "It's the heat."

Margaret put her hand on top of Fran's. "Them are hives. Plain as day," she whispered.

"They're all right."

Margaret watched as Fran rang up each item and put it into a sack. "Have you thought more about finding him a colored home?"

"I promised his . . ."

"Good Lord, Fran! It was a promise to a dying woman. Now whoever's doing this is going to pick off your animals one by one until you get that boy out of your house." She dug through her pocketbook and handed Fran some money. "You are making yourself sick over this. Look at you. You haven't slept and your arms and neck are covered with hives. You need to take better care of yourself. You've got another youngin to think about."

"I promised his mama."

Margaret shook her head. "Don't neglect your own youngins, Fran. Talk some sense into her, will you, Henry?" She picked up her sack of groceries and walked out the door.

That night as we got ready for bed I watched as Fred turned round and round on the rug we'd put

on the porch for him. "Mama, can Fred Dog
sleep inside in the kitchen tonight?"

"No."

"But Mama, he's . . ."

"Animals don't sleep inside the house, Jane."

"But he's so small," I said, hoping Mama
would understand.

She sighed and shook her head. "Put him right
inside the door but that's it. He ain't allowed in
the rest of the house."

I opened the door to the kitchen for Fred but
he wouldn't budge. I slapped my leg and squatted
down to him but he wouldn't move. I propped
the door open and nudged him with my foot; he
stiffened his front legs. "Go on! Get in there." I
picked him up and set him inside the kitchen. He
ran for the open door but I slammed it shut before he could escape.

Milo climbed into bed and turned to face the
window. Mama pulled the sheet up to his neck.
"Sleep good, Milo. I'll see you in the morning."

"Ma'am," Milo said, turning his head to look
at her. "Jane said them men that was here yesterday was after money from your dead husband."

I felt my heart flip but I couldn't catch Mama's
eyes. She sat down next to Milo. "That's right."

"Did they kill that cow?"

"I don't know."

He looked up at her. "Do you think they did?"

She was quiet. "I don't know. I hope not."

Milo turned and faced the window and Mama walked to my bed, pulling the sheet up to my and John's necks. The patches under her eyes grew darker every day. "Night, Mama." She forced a smile, closed the door behind her, and for the first time in my life I heard her lock the doors before going to bed.

Each evening I took every precaution against getting up in the middle of the night to go to the outhouse, but my bladder told me there was no way around it that night. I threw the covers off and tiptoed through the front room. I didn't bring the coal oil lamp. It was too much trouble. I ran across the backyard and pulled open the outhouse door, banging on it to scare off any snake or animal that may have gotten inside. I stood on my toes and pulled down my under-pants. I was convinced spiders clung to webs on the outhouse ceiling so I covered my head to keep them from getting in my hair. I hummed to let animals know to stay away, and then I ran out the door for the house, catching my breath when I got inside the front room. I walked back toward our bedroom but stopped when I heard Mama. I crept down the hall toward her door and heard what sounded like crying. I paused, wondering what to do, and then headed for my room again before stopping. What if something was wrong with the baby?

I pushed open the door. "Are you sick, Mama?" I heard her move.

"No, Jane. I'm all right. Go back to bed."

"Is the baby sick?"

"No. Go on now."

I turned to leave. "But I thought I heard you crying." She didn't respond. I waited, hoping she'd say something but she was quiet. "Are you scared, Mama?"

There was a long pause before she answered. "Yes, Jane. I am."

I'd never done it before but I walked to her bed and pulled back the covers, sliding in next to her. I pulled the blankets close to her neck and lay down, putting my hand on her shoulder. "Everything's gonna be all right, Mama. I promise." I kept my hand there throughout the night.

Fran slept little; the slightest noise made her jump. she finally got up before sunrise and carried a lamp into the kitchen, striking a match to light the stove. The sound of something on the porch made her heart quicken and Fred stood to his feet, pressing his nose to the door. She reached to the side of the icebox where she kept a rifle. She opened a cabinet and pulled out an old matchbox, retrieving two shells from inside. Her hands shook as she loaded the shells into the rifle chamber. She moved to the door and eased the curtain to the side. Perspiration broke out on her palms when she made out the form of a man on the porch. She cocked the rifle and threw open the door. "I swear to God I will shoot you right here!"

Henry stood and raised his hands in the air. "Lord have mercy! You need to work on your greeting, Fran."

She put the gun down and air rushed from her lungs. "What in the world are you doing, Henry?"

"I'm making sure your livestock makes it through the night."

She sank into the swing on the porch. "Seems we got it backward around here. Dogs sleep in the house and people sleep on the porch."

Henry fell onto the swing beside her. "And get greeted with a rifle in their face. Don't forget that part." He stretched and moaned in pain.

"Does Loretta know you're here?"

He arched his back and groaned. "It was her idea!"

She helped him inside the kitchen and sat at the table. "Look what's happening around here, Henry. All of this over a little colored boy."

He sat across from her. "It'll get better, Fran."

"Can you promise that?"

"No."

She nodded. She could always count on Henry to be truthful.

Chapter
SEVEN

We worked at the Cannons' for two more weeks and in mid-August the tobacco was ready to cut. It would take all of us working right up through Labor Day to bring in the two acres to cure. On the morning we were going to start cutting the tobacco John and Milo and I ate a huge breakfast before heading to the Cannon farm.

It had been more than two weeks since Mama told me to walk the boys along the road instead of the tracks but we were running late. We'd never cut tobacco before and we were excited to start our day. By the time we milked the cows, fed the pigs, and gathered the eggs it was getting later and hotter by the minute. I knew Mama would be angry if she knew we had walked along the railroad but I figured that what she didn't know wouldn't hurt her. I led the boys down the embankment. "You said Mama don't want us on the tracks," John said.

"She don't care this morning. Besides, Beef's house is that way and we go this way."

He pulled the pilot's cap onto his head. "Why don't Mama care this morning?"

"John, just hush up."

"Youngins are supposed to listen to their mamas." I snapped my head to see Beef standing ten feet from us. I held tighter to Milo's hand and walked past Beef. "You hear me?" He jumped onto the track behind us and grabbed John's arm. "You all listen when I talk to you."

I smelled liquor on him and pulled John from his grasp. "We hear you. We're just running late to work." I held to John's hand and kept walking.

Beef pulled Milo toward him. "What's this little nigger boy doing working?" He flicked Milo's ear. "What are you doing, Wingnut?"

I didn't care what Henry said. I couldn't see a puddle of tears next to Beef. I jumped over the rail and knocked his hand off Milo. "Leave him alone, you fat . . ." Then in a moment that stood still on that hot August morning I let out the granddaddy of all curse words—a word that I had heard my daddy use a hundred times but one that made my mother flinch every time he said it. My blood raced as soon as it came out of my mouth, and the back of Beef's enormous hand smacked me across the face.

"What'd you say to me?" His chest was heaving. I fell onto the tracks and saw drops of blood splatter onto the white rocks below me. I had awakened something dark and angry in Beef and I could feel my heart beating hard inside my chest.

John screamed when I fell. He wanted to yell for help but the words were at the back of his throat and his tongue couldn't connect with the roof of his mouth. He sputtered out what he could. "N-n-n-n-no!" He lunged and sank his teeth into Beef's meaty thumb. I watched from the ground and yelled for John to stop. Beef wrapped a hand around John's head and threw him to the ground. John landed on his arm and groaned. Milo kicked Beef and Beef grabbed Milo's shoulders, shaking him. John and I cried out back and forth for Beef to stop.

"Stop it," I screamed. I jumped onto Beef's

back and bit down on his ear, drawing blood. He yelled and threw me off, knocking me across the face again, this time clipping my eye with his knuckles. I raised my legs to kick him away but before I could he landed with a thud beside me. I looked up and saw Ruby holding an iron skillet.

"I won't let him hurt ya."

I jumped to my feet, looking at Beef's broad back lying beside the tracks. I was shaking. "Did you kill him?"

She kicked his foot off the tracks. "He's too mean to kill. He'll come to when that lump on his head quits hurtin'." She reached into her dress pocket and put something in Milo's hand. Addy's necklace dangled from his palm. "I believe this belonged to your mama. It was shining in the sun one day way over yonder on the tracks. I used to watch her walk to and from the store and she always waved at me. She waved at me real nice." Milo looked up at her but didn't say anything. "You all better get on now." That was the first time I'd seen Ruby smile.

John couldn't go to the Cannons'; his arm was dangling at his side like one of the fish we'd string up on Sunday afternoons. We ran down the tracks to Doc Langley's house and although we begged him not to he called Mama at the store. While we waited for her Doc wrapped John's arm and set it in a sling. John couldn't have been more proud when Mama arrived. "That's some kind of contraption, ain't it?"

"He'll need to wear this for a few weeks," Doc said. John was thrilled.

Mama watched as Doc examined me, careful as he touched the eye that was tender and red and tended to my busted lip. "No bones are broken in her face, Fran. You'll need to keep ice on this eye though. That swelling's going to take a while to go down. It'll turn every color there is." He handed her a small pouch filled with powder. "Mix a half teaspoon of this in a cup of water for each of them to help with pain."

Mama nodded and we walked to the store. She hadn't said anything to us since she arrived at Doc's. I was hoping she'd just let us have it and get it over with. "Are you all right?" she asked the three of us. John and I nodded. "Milo, are you all right?"

"Yes, ma'am."

"Can you go to work, Jane?" I nodded. "John, you want to go?"

He held up his gimp arm. "You better believe it!" He had a sling to show off and war stories about how he was lucky enough to get it.

"Milo? You want to go?" Milo nodded and we

walked farther on in silence. "One of you all need to tell me how you got into a fight with Beef and I don't want to hear lies. You understand me?"

John was the first to explain. "Jane called him a fat . . ." And he belted out the granddaddy of all curse words.

Mama stopped and looked at me. "What did you say, Jane?" John blurted out the word again and she spun toward him. "I heard you the first time, John." She turned to me. "Why would you say such a thing?"

"He yanked on Milo and called him Wingnut."

"What were you doing on the tracks in the first place?"

"We were going to be late for the first day of cutting tobacco and it was so doggone hot that we couldn't walk along the road. We'd be dripping all the way down into our shoes by the time we got there. The tracks were easier."

"They were a whole lot easier." Sarcasm laced her tone. "Why do you think I told you to stay off the tracks?" I didn't answer. "You know as well as I do that Beef walks down to the creek same as everybody else. He don't just stay by the tracks that are by his house. You're lucky Ruby was there. Who knows what else that fool would have done?" Henry and Loretta watched as Mama marched us to the sink in the back of the store.

She took down the lye soap from the holder and held it in front of me. "Open," she said. I opened my mouth and she stuck the thick, gray bar between my teeth. "Close." I wrapped my lips around it and she positioned me to face the wall. "Filthy talk ain't fit to be used on anybody. Not even Beef." I gagged and heard John snicker. Mama pushed him and Milo to the front of the store and left me there for several minutes. She was shaking and Loretta put an arm around her.

"They're okay, Fran." Mama nodded, holding back tears. When she couldn't stand the sound of my choking any longer she pulled the soap out of my mouth and twisted the water on for me. I bent over into the sink and turned my face up to the faucet, letting the water wash over my tongue, scraping the soap off with my fingers.

"You can tell the Cannons about what happened but don't you tell anybody else that Beef did this to you."

"But, Mama," John said, lifting his wounded arm.

"Not a word. Louise goes to school with you all. What will people think when they hear her daddy did this?"

"But what do we tell everybody?" John asked.

"You'll think of something."

Henry drove us to the Cannons'. Joe and Del were already at work when we got there. Henry explained what happened and Joe knelt down and gathered us to him like chicks to a hen. John rattled on and on about our run-in with Beef but I leaned my head on Joe's shoulder, feeling his hand pat my shoulder. We laid the story out bare for the Cannons but for anyone else who asked what happened to John we told them the only thing we could think of—he got hit over the head in Greeneville . . . and fell on his arm.

"Are you all up for work?" Joe asked.

"I got this lame arm," John said, lifting the sling. "But I'll do all I can with the good one I got left." I rolled my eyes. He was going to be impossible to live with for the next few weeks.

"I'm ready," Milo said. "Let's bring it in." Joe rubbed the top of Milo's head and we followed him into the patch.

Del took a small S-shaped knife and cut a stalk from the top of a tobacco plant to about six inches from the bottom and handed it off to John, Milo, and me. "Careful of them leaves," he said. "They need to be full without tears or holes. Keep 'em pretty." The three of us speared the stalk over a stick and when we had four to five stalks on a stick, either Joe or Del helped us carry it to the wagon. We lifted the stick as high as we could over our heads to one of them on the wagon bed; our arms shook under the weight. Joe or Del grabbed hold of the end and hung it on the wooden bar of the wagon. We tramped back to the patch and began spearing again. I looked out over the field. At this pace it would take us forever to bring the rest of it in. "I can't work any faster because of my lame arm," John said.

"Would you hush up about that arm!"

"Well, don't holler at me to work faster. I'm doing all a man can do when he's got a lame arm." I walked away from him.

I didn't want to think about Joe leaving Morgan Hill again for Atlanta, but I knew that once the tobacco was in he'd go and I'd rarely see him. "Joe, you like living in Atlanta?"

"It's all right."

"Don't you miss Morgan Hill?"

"Sure I do."

I stopped my work. "Then why don't you come on back?"

He took the handkerchief from his back pocket and wiped his face. "Because I got me a good job there and I promised my buddy that I'd work with him. I can make more money there in a year than I can in two years working this farm."

"When you gonna leave again?"

He handed me a stalk. "Soon as we get all this in the barn."

I nodded but in my heart I prayed he would never leave again.

John was so tired that night that he forgot to ask me to look for the bogeyman under his bed. He and Milo were asleep by the time I used the outhouse and came back inside. I don't even know if they said good night to Mama. I crawled in next to John and felt my arms shaking; they were still trembling long after we had stopped work. I had never been so tired.

A week went by and although we'd made headway I'd look out over the field each morning and know we were in trouble. John and Milo and I were exhausted. We were working as hard as we could to help Joe and Del, but there was no way we could bring all the tobacco in before school started and by then it'd be past its prime.

I rolled over one night and watched as clouds rolled past the moon out my window. I flopped over onto my side when a flash darted past

Milo's window. Fred Dog began to bark and I jumped up and sat next to Milo on his bed, watching as a truck I didn't recognize parked in front of the barn.

John pushed his way in beside us. "Who is that?"

"I don't know," I said. Two people made their way to the house but it was too dark; we couldn't see who they were. We sat still as they walked onto the porch and knocked on the screen door. I heard Mama shuffle into the kitchen and the door creaked open. The lamp she carried shed just enough light for us to see the strangers' faces.

"Them's colored people," John said.

"Shhh," I said, pressing closer to the window screen.

"Miz Gable?"

"Yes."

"I'm Reverend Harold Alden." He looked at the woman with him. "This here's my wife, Esther." The woman smiled and stepped closer to her husband's side. "I'm sorry to come to your home, uninvited, Miz Gable, but we couldn't find a phone number."

"We ain't got a phone."

"We ain't got one neither. Not at home, least ways, but at the church we do. We don't mean to bother you as it's getting late into the evening but one of our oldest members at church took bad sick. We just now left her. Could you spare us some time, Miz Gable?"

Mama nodded and Reverend Alden grabbed the door from her, directing his wife inside. The screen door snapped closed and John and I scrambled, working at the screws that held our window screen in place. We loosened them and pushed the screen out, catching it before it fell against the house. We tumbled out the window one at a time and crept to the porch. Fred barked and I grabbed his nose, hushing him. John and Milo squatted beneath the window and I hovered near the door. "Would you like some coffee?" Mama asked.

"Please don't bother, Miz Gable," Mrs. Alden said. "Thank you, though." I put my hands on the porch and leaned closer to the screen door, peering inside. Mama was sitting in a chair near the door with her back to it. I sighed with relief; I knew she wouldn't be able to hear us with her bad ear closest to the door. I moved my head to look past Mama to the Aldens. They looked familiar.

"Miz Gable, I'm the minister at the Mount Zion Baptist Church in Greeneville. Me and Esther have two grown boys and another one left at

home. We heard what happened to the Turners
on the radio and came out to the funeral." That's
where I'd seen them. "We are terrible sorry for
the loss in this community." Mama nodded, listening. John lost his balance and rolled forward
into Milo, pushing him against the house. I
snapped my head from the door and leaned
against the wall, shoving my finger to my lips to
quiet John. I sat still, straining to hear if Mama
or the Aldens had heard the commotion.

"Miz Gable, it's been said that you have
agreed to raise the boy."

"That's right." I crawled to the door again and
lifted my head to see inside.

Reverend Alden shifted in his chair and I noticed cow manure on the sides of his shoes. "Me
and Esther have been talking ever since the funeral and we ain't got much, Miz Gable, but the
Lord has always provided and we always been
fed and had a place to live and clothes to wear.
And we been able to marry off two boys and
send them up north for work so we got us a bedroom that's empty." Milo didn't move. "Miz
Gable, we done talked about this and want you
to know that we'll raise that boy if you want."
Mama remained quiet.

"You can tell us if we're stepping into a place
we don't belong," Mrs. Alden said. "But we just

wanted to come and let you know that we're here if you think the boy wants to be raised in a colored home. We're good people, Miz Gable. We'd be good to the boy."

Mama nodded. "I can see that, Miz Alden."

"We can come back in a few days," Reverend Alden said. "I know it's getting late so we can come talk with you again another time."

"But maybe he would like to come to our house," Mrs. Alden said. My heart pounded; we should have been scurrying back through the window but I couldn't move. I had to hear what was happening. "He could meet our boy and see where we live. We could come get him one day and have him over for part of the day. You could come, too, Miz Gable. You and your youngins."

It was quiet so I leaned closer to hear how Mama would respond. "It'd probably be best if just Milo visited with you. This needs to be his decision." I glanced back at Milo but he didn't look at me. I ran toward the bedroom window and heard Milo and John behind me. We helped Milo in first and then John stepped into my hands and he pulled himself in, stretching his hands toward me. I lifted myself up and John and Milo pulled me into Milo's bed as the screen door creaked open. We fell and lay flat on the bed, careful not to be seen.

"The screen! The screen!" John whispered.

"She won't notice," I said, hushing him.

Mama held on to the oil lamp and walked Reverend and Mrs. Alden to their truck. We lifted our heads and saw Mama standing alone, watching the Aldens as they drove down the driveway. There are times when you know more than you should and as I watched Milo, still and unmoving, I knew that we'd heard too much. As kind as they seemed I wished I hadn't known anything about Reverend and Mrs. Alden.

I opened my eyes the next morning but couldn't move my arms. My whole body ached. John and Milo and I were quiet milking the cows. None of us wanted to bring up what we'd heard the night before. I couldn't see Milo from where I was milking Flo but I heard his small voice. "Is your mama sending me away?"

"Don't worry about nothing," I said.

"But it'd be better for everybody if she did."

I couldn't answer. I hoped that the Aldens would just go away if we didn't think or talk about them.

Late that afternoon as we climbed the embankment for home we saw a car we didn't recognize speeding up our driveway. We scrambled around the house, trying to see the driver. John was in front, running at full speed, when he stopped in his tracks. "Run! Run for your lives." He charged toward us waving his arms. "It's Aunt Dora." I screamed and grabbed Milo's hand as we ran back toward the tracks.

Dora stuck her head out the car window. "Angel darlin's! Come back. It's your Aunt Dora." She had seen us.

"Keep running!" John said, yelling. "Run before it's too late."

Dora honked the horn. "Come on back, you all. It's your sweet Aunt Dora."

"It's no use," I said. "We've been caught." John stopped as if he'd been shot in the back and fell to the ground. Milo looked at me and I held his shoulder. "When she comes for you, turn your face as quick as a wink."

Dora stepped out of the car and opened her arms as she ran to us. "Run right into these arms so I can love on you." I walked to Dora, positioning my face for the best angle when she moved in for the kiss. "Janie darlin'," she said, grabbing my head. I couldn't move. How could I dodge the direct contact kiss if I couldn't move my face? She pulled me to her and planted a red, moist kiss on my lips. I reeled backward and Dora moved for John. He was still crumpled on the ground. She got down on her hands and knees and peered over his head. "Peek-a-boo!" She covered her eyes and laughed. "Peek-a-boo!" John threw his arms over his face and Dora picked them up and kissed him on the mouth. He jumped to his feet and ran his entire face back and forth over his arm.

Dora giggled and turned to look at Milo. He couldn't move. His feet were concrete. I leaned in to him. "Quick as a wink."

Dora stood in front of him and extended her hand. "You must be Milo." Milo shook her hand and Dora knelt in front of him. "I'm so glad to meet you."

Mama was surprised to see Dora but she set a place for her at supper. She served pinto beans made with fatback, fried potatoes, green beans, onions, and a skillet full of corn bread. Dora spooned out the chunk of fatback and flopped it onto her plate, tearing it apart with her fingers. She pressed a greasy finger into the end of Milo's nose. "You're just as handsome as handsome can be! How old are you?"

"Six."

Dora tore into the piece of fatback. "Six years old and just as handsome as handsome can be. And my other two angels have gotten so big since I last seen them." Dora pinched John's cheek and left a mark of bean soup and grease on his face. He huffed and rolled his eyes until Mama snapped her fingers under the table. Dora reached for my nose and I lifted the skillet of corn bread in front of her. She broke off a huge piece. I smiled at John, confident that I had avoided her wet clutch, but then felt a cold, oily finger on the tip of my nose. "Thank you, darlin' baby." John and Milo and I ran from the table when we were done eating. The cows needed their evening milking and we were more than happy to get to the barn and away from Dora's slippery touch.

"I didn't know you were coming," Fran said, warming water on the stove to wash the dishes.

"I won't stay long."

Fran put washing powder into the basin and collected the plates off the table. "You can stay as long as you want, Dora."

Dora stood and poured hot water into the basin. "Let me wash them, Fran. You can sit." Fran hadn't sat in years and couldn't start now. She poured leftover beans into a bowl and put a plate over the top of it, setting it inside the icebox. She wrapped the corn bread in waxed paper and dried the dishes as she listened to Dora talk about her job. Dora asked countless questions about the baby and discussed the weather; she actually brought the weather up a second time when the conversation waned. They stepped outside and Fred led them as they walked toward the barn.

"Does he ask about his mama and daddy?"

"Some. He ain't talked about them too much."

"He will," Dora said. She stopped and leaned against her truck. "What were they like?"

"They were good people." Fran shook her head, looking toward the barn. "I'll never understand it. Never, never, never." She sighed and put her hands on her belly. "I need to get on up to the barn and help finish that milking." She stepped away from the car but Dora stopped her.

"Fran. I've been doing some thinking. It doesn't make sense for me to take the bus to work every day and leave my car sitting in the driveway." Fran stepped toward her but Dora put up her hand. "I've known you for a long time, Fran, and I know what you're apt to say but I want you to listen to me. You got three kids under your roof and another one on the way, and from what I hear it's getting too dangerous to walk down the tracks these days."

"We ain't even seen Beef since it happened. He's too embarrassed to come around. For all he knows he thinks three youngins whooped him. He won't . . ."

Dora held up her hand. "You need a car a whole lot more than I do." Fran shook her head. "Please listen! I take the bus to work and I'm able to walk to the grocery. I don't need this car."

"No, no, no," Fran said.

"I've made up my mind, Fran."

"So have I. There ain't no reason to talk about it."

"Fran, I know how my brother was and I know the kind of man he wasn't. I never want to be like him. I never want to be the kind of person he was. I'm sorry for what happened in this house for the last ten years, and I'm ashamed that somebody in my family was responsible for all of it."

Fran shuffled her feet and looked at the ground. "You're not one thing like Lonnie and you ain't got nothing to be sorry about, Dora. What happened in this house ain't one bit your fault and you don't need to feel that you got to do something about it."

"I don't feel that I have to do something, Fran, but I *want* to do something because I can. I'm in the time of my life when I can do this. I live a real simple life in Cleveland. It's just me and this car that I rarely use. And you're in the time of your life where you could get a whole lot more use out of this thing than I will." She looked toward the barn and watched as the children milked the cows. "I don't have to do this, Fran, but I sure do want to." She paused and smiled. "Besides, I figure if I keep taking the bus I'm bound to find a husband one day."

Dora and Mama were up early the next morning. I wakened and caught bits and pieces of what they said. Mama was going to take Dora to the crossroads to catch the bus but Dora wouldn't hear of it, not while we were still sleeping. "I'll walk to the store," Dora said. "Some old man will be loafin' this morning who'll give me a ride."

"I wish you'd stay longer, Dora."

"I need to get back to work and it's a long bus ride."

I heard the kitchen door close, jumped out of bed, and threw open the bedroom door. I ran through the house in my underpants and undershirt. "Mama, where's Dora going?"

"To the crossroads."

I ran onto the porch and saw her car. "Why ain't she driving her car?"

"She gave us her car, Jane." Neither she nor Dora had said anything about it last night. Shame stabbed me. How could Dora give us her car after all the hateful thoughts I'd had about her and the degrees I always went to to avoid her? I ran down the steps of the porch and leaped over the embankment.

I screamed after her. "Aunt Dora! Wait!"

"Janie angel! What in the world are you doing out here in your underclothes?"

I caught up to her and she knelt down in front of me. "Where you going, Aunt Dora?"

"I need to get on home before old Mister No-Hair fires me."

"When you coming back?"

She smiled and kissed me. I didn't even attempt to pull away. "Someday. Maybe after your mama has that baby." She squeezed my arm and held on to my hand. "You better get on back now and get some clothes on before Sheriff Dutton arrests you." She stood and picked up her suitcase. "Take good care of your mama, Jane."

I nodded and she walked away from me. "Aunt Dora!" She turned back.

"Thank you!" She smiled and blew me a kiss and I watched as she rounded the bend and disappeared.

That morning as we finished the milking I helped Mama tighten all the lids on the milk cans. John and Milo were busy running in and out of our new car. I wanted Mama to talk about the Aldens but I didn't know how to bring them up. "School'll be starting soon," I said. She wasn't paying attention. "I bet Milo will be excited to go to school with us."

She stopped her work and looked at me. "Jane, you need to know that Milo ain't able to go to school with you and John."

I felt sick. I just knew she was going to tell me she'd decided to let Milo live with the Aldens. "Why not?"

"Because it's a white school. There ain't no coloreds in it."

I hadn't seen that coming. "But there ain't never been coloreds in Morgan Hill to go to school before."

She turned the last lid and looked at me. "I know that."

"How will he learn if he ain't in school? Did you ask Mister Jeffers?"

"He can't do anything about it. Milo could go to Greeneville."

I felt blood rush to my head. "But he can't go into Greeneville. He lives here, Mama!" She wiped her hands on a rag and dabbed it to her forehead. "Are you sending him away?"

She turned to me. "What have you been hearing?"

"I heard them colored folk say they'd take

Milo. Are you sending him away so he can live with them and go to a colored school?"

She looked toward John and Milo. "I don't know."

"You promised Addy!"

She spun toward me. "I know what I promised his mama! But twelve years from now he's still going to be a young man living in this home, this *white* home, Jane, and I been up nights studying on what that's going to do to him. He might be better off with them folks."

I stared at her back and watched her breathe. Maybe she was right but the thought made me angry. "Just cause them people are colored don't mean they could take care of him better than us."

She kept her back to me. "Go on in the house and get ready for work, Jane."

I felt my heart sink. "Are you sending him away?"

"Go on, Jane."

Chapter
EIGHT

We made our way to the Cannons' and the sight of all the tobacco that was left made me hurt all over. John, Milo, and I trudged toward the patch but stopped when we saw Henry's truck pull up the drive. He honked and then he and Loretta got out. I'd never been so happy to see anyone in my life.

He pulled a knife from his truck and walked toward us, waving it like he was one of the Three Musketeers. "Maxine said on the radio this morning to expect rain in three days, Joe. So we better make hay when the sun's shining." *Make hay when the sun's shining* was a common phrase used by the farmers in Morgan Hill. If the sun was shining you got as much work done as possible. Everybody knew that tobacco brought more money in at auction if the leaves weren't muddy or spoiled by sitting on wet ground. If we wanted to get top dollar we needed to get the tobacco in the barn before the rain came. Pete and Charlotte Fletcher pulled in next to Henry's truck. "Mornin', everybody," Pete said, lifting his knife off the front seat.

Later in the day Hoby Kane and Otis and Nona Dodd showed up and even Mama herself. She closed the store early, hanging a *Bringing in Tobacco* sign on the door. If anybody thought Otis and Nona were too old or Hoby was too crippled to help, nobody said a word. Hoby reached in his pocket and offered a handful of lemon drops to John and Milo and me to help keep us going. "I won't tell your mama," he said, winking at us. When word got out that the Cannons were bringing in their tobacco before the storm hit, Jeb Hancock, Cal Dodson, and Dody Gumm turned out for work. Although he'd made peace with work ten years earlier, even admitted lazy man Gabbie Doakes showed up. Trucks barreled into the driveway each morning and after a few cups of Helen's coffee the crew made their way into the field.

We broke up into teams of three each morning and I was on Henry and Loretta's team. John was with Cal Dodson and Del. Milo worked with Mama and Joe. Milo had worked so much with Joe on the farm that they didn't have to talk to get the work done. Milo knew what Joe wanted before he asked. My mother was at ease working in the patch. She fell into work beside Joe as if they were made to do it together. I couldn't remember her and Daddy doing anything together.

In three days the tobacco that Willie Dean and Addy had planted was cut and hanging in the barn. Milo stared at it hanging from the rafters. There it was: the reason his parents had driven to Morgan Hill from Mississippi. It would hang there at least two months to cure before going to auction.

After I got the money from the Pet Milk Company the next morning I walked back to the house, going over the conversation I had with Mama about the Aldens again and again in my mind. We hadn't spoken about it any more but her silence told me she was going to send Milo away. Heavy, silver clouds hung low in the sky. I felt raindrops hit the top of my head and looked up; another drop hit my cheek and I hurried before the clouds burst open. I walked past Mama who was doing laundry on the porch and threw the money down on the kitchen table. I walked to the chicken coop for John and Milo; we needed to pick beans before the rain hit. John was spreading feed on the ground. "Where's Milo?" John shrugged and spread the feed out farther beyond him, kicking at the chickens to clear a path as he walked. "Where's he at, John?"

"I don't know. I thought he was with you in the barn." I walked to the back of the chicken coop and made my way through and then around the barn, calling for Milo. I crossed over the driveway and looked into the garden, hoping he was already picking the beans, but he was nowhere to be found. I looked in the cellar and pulled open the outhouse door. I slammed it shut and ran down the embankment, looking both ways on the track. I stumbled toward the house.

"Is Milo in the house?" Mama's bad ear was toward me. "Mama, is Milo in the house?" I asked, louder this time. She looked up from the washboard. "Milo's run off again."

She dried her hands as she brushed past me. "Did you look in the barn?"

I nodded. "He ain't in there. I been up and down the driveway, in the cellar, the garden, everywhere."

She ran down the porch steps and walked toward the back of the house. "When did you last see him?" she asked, a mixture of fear and anger in her voice.

"When we were finishing up milking."

"Did you check the tracks?" I nodded. "You and John head toward the creek and look for him. I'll go to the Cannons' and see if he went there. He couldn't get too far." She eased down the embankment and I could see her running along the tracks, calling Milo's name. John and I ran toward the creek.

By the time Fran reached the Cannons' a steady sprinkle was falling. Helen saw her running and opened the front door. "Fran Gable, what in the world are you doing out in the rain?"

"Is Milo here?"

"I've not seen him," Helen said. Joe stepped in beside his mother. "Milo's gone," she said. He grabbed his cap off the hook hanging in the kitchen. "Why would he run off like this?"

"Cause he's so lonesome that he don't know what to do with himself," Joe said, pulling the cap onto his head. "Fran, you don't need to be running around when a storm's about to hit. Stay here with Mother. Me and Pop will find him."

She stepped toward the porch but Helen touched her arm. "Fran, let Joe and Del look for him. They'll bring him home."

Fran stopped and watched as Joe and Del searched in opposite directions. "I'll call Henry and Loretta," she said, reaching for the phone. "Maybe he went down to the store."

Henry hung up the phone and left Loretta alone while he searched the roads in his truck.

John and I ran to the creek but Milo wasn't there. Lightning flashed and the clouds opened, forcing buckets of water on us. We screamed his name louder, hoping he'd hear us over the pounding rain. "What'd he run away for?" John asked, leaping across the rocks.

"I don't know."

"It don't make a lick of sense why he run off." I ignored John and ran faster, careful to keep my footing once I reached the tracks. "You reckon he run off for good?"

"I don't know, John," I said, hoping the tone of my voice would stop his endless questions.

He crossed his arms and drew his hands up under his armpits. "Why the devil would he run off?"

I stopped running and turned on him. "Cause he knows Mama wants to send him off to them colored people." Rain dripped off the flaps of John's pilot's cap as he stared at me. I shook my head, running up the embankment to the Cannons'.

John and I waited on the porch, watching for Joe or Del or Henry to show up with Milo, but they never did. An hour passed when Del, soggy and soaked to the bone, was seen walking through the pastures west of the Cannon property. As he got closer we could see him shake his head. Joe came back thirty minutes later. He'd walked into town and spoken with Cal Dodson and Olive Harper but neither had seen Milo. Mama stood up from the kitchen table and watched the rain pool in the yard. "Maybe Henry spotted him," Helen said. Mama nodded.

But Henry hadn't spotted Milo. He had driven miles in every direction without seeing him or anyone else for that matter. The rain kept everyone inside. Mama sat and rubbed her face in her hands. "We'll find him, Fran," Henry said. "He ain't able to get too far in this rain. He's probably hiding in somebody's barn and when the rain lets up he'll come on out." Mama didn't respond. "I'll take Jane and John back to your house in case he decided to go back there."

When we got home John and I ran through the barn again, hoping Milo had already come back. Henry reached for two towels out of the kitchen and threw them over my head and then John's. John sat on the edge of the porch, letting the water from the gutter rush over his legs.

"He ran off cause we ain't been good to him, Henry," I said.

Henry rubbed the towel into my hair. "That's enough of that. Milo ran off because he's eat up with grief. But once he's had time to think he'll come on back."

I didn't say anything. Thunder cracked above us and shook the house. "Mama's thinking about sending Milo to live with some colored folks in Greeneville."

Henry worked the towel over my arms and legs. "What folk?"

"Some preacher and his wife. They came to the funeral, then showed up at the house the other night and talked with Mama."

"She told you?" I shook my head. "Then how do you know?"

"Me and John heard 'em talking."

"Did Milo hear, too?" I shrugged my shoulders. "Did Milo hear your mama talking to them people?"

"I believe he did."

"You *believe*?"

"He did."

"I don't reckon it'd do any good to tell you two that it ain't nice to eavesdrop."

"She's gonna send him away, Henry, and she promised Addy she'd raise him."

"You don't know that."

"I know Mama."

"I don't believe you do, Pretty Girl. If you did, then you'd know that your mama's going to do what's right." Henry was wrong; I didn't know that. I didn't think Mama knew it, either.

"You think Addy and Willie Dean can see us?" I asked. "You think they see that we lost their boy?"

He wrapped the towel tighter around me. "God sees him."

"Will he tell Milo to come on back?"

He rested his chin on top of my head. "I'm sure He's working on him. If He goes out of his way to find one lost sheep then I bet anything that He'll do whatever it takes to bring home one boy lost in a storm."

Helen spent the rest of the morning on the phone. She left word for Sheriff Dutton to watch for Milo, and an hour later he pulled into the Cannon drive to see if Milo had returned. He promised to do what he could to find him and drove away, mud flying from beneath the wheels of his car. Fran paced on the porch and watched water drain off the roof of the barn. Thunder cracked, sounding as if it had rolled right over the face of Widow's Mountain.

"We thought it would have let up by now," Joe said, joining her on the porch. "But Henry's right. Milo's probably huddled up in a barn somewhere. He ain't running around in this." She nodded and turned away before Joe could see the tears rimming her eyes. "He's all right, Fran. He's a smart boy. He's found some place dry to stay till this lets up." Joe stepped in front of her, lifting her face. A tear fell onto her cheek and she swiped at it with her hand, then crossed her arms in front of her. "Fran, this ain't your fault."

She put her hands on the porch railing and lowered her head, looking at the floorboards. "Well, it ain't his fault, Joe. He's just a little boy. He ran off cause he don't want to be in my house."

"That's not true."

"I ain't given that boy one reason to stay and truth is I don't know if he should. A colored family from Greeneville came to the house and said they could take Milo." She looked up at Joe. "They could raise him."

"What did you tell them?"

"They said Milo could go to their house. Meet their boy. I thought it was a good idea. After he meets them then we'll all have time to think."

"What will you tell them when you've had time to think?"

She shook her head and turned before Joe could see the tears fall. "He needs to decide, Joe. But he knows. He's not blind or deaf to what's been happening since he came, and I sure ain't made that house a home for him. He knows he's better off wandering around out there in the rain than stuck inside that house with me."

Joe leaned against the railing, facing her. "Fran, he ran off because he's so sad that he don't know what to do. He didn't run off because of you or because you told him about them folks. He ran off cause he don't know what to do with the pain that's just ripping at him." She cupped her hands on the railing and rested her forehead in them. Joe put his hands on her shoulders and pulled her up to face him. "He knows you're a good soul, Fran. His mama knew that. I have *always* known that." She looked at him and he took hold of her hand. "As long as I've known you you ain't been nothing but a good, decent person." Tears rolled down her face because for the first time in years a man had touched her in kindness and spoken to her with tenderness but she couldn't respond. She wasn't used to anything resembling affection from a man so she shrank away, wiping the tears from her cheeks. She'd been standing on her own for a long time and she didn't know how to rely on someone now. Joe caught her eye but she wouldn't look at him.

"Me and Pop are going back out," he said. "Hopefully, we'll find him this time."

They didn't find him, and although Henry and I had left John at the house and driven to one house and then another looking through barns and well houses and any outbuildings we could see, Milo was nowhere to be found.

There was a long stretching away of time that day; hours crept by with no news from anyone in town. We nibbled on chicken and pinto beans out of the icebox for supper and when we finished Henry drove us back to the Cannons'. Mama's face was dark. It had been a long day for all of us. "There's still a couple of hours of light left," Henry said. "We can sweep across the pastures and roads again before nightfall." Joe and Del nodded and grabbed their jackets. John and I ran and climbed into Henry's truck.

• • •

Fran stepped onto the porch and ran down the steps for the railroad tracks. "Fran," Helen said. "You ain't got no business out in this rain in your condition. Something could happen to you or the baby." Fran started down the embankment.

"Fran," Joe said, grabbing her arm. "Stay in the house with Mother. It'll be getting dark soon."

She pushed wet hair off her face. "You're right. In a little while we won't be able to see beyond the porch. Then what, Joe? What happens to a little colored boy wandering about on the dark roads or in the hills?" Joe didn't answer. "I'm going."

She continued down the embankment and Joe jumped down in front of her. He offered her his hand and helped her to the tracks that were slippery with water. They walked into town but everything was quiet. She found the key Henry kept hidden under the sacks of feed on the porch and opened the store, hoping Milo somehow got in after Loretta locked up for the day but he wasn't there.

She tried to lock the door and felt her throat tighten. Her hands shook; she couldn't turn the key; it was slick in her hands. She dropped it and picked it up, trying again but the lock wasn't turning. She slapped her palm against the door. "This stupid thing!"

"We'll find him, Fran," Joe said, taking the key. He slid it into the lock and turned it till it clicked.

They ran back to the railroad and Fran stopped to wipe her face with the sleeve of her dress. She called Milo's name, raising her head so her voice carried up to the hills. Her heart beat faster and she ran on top of the railroad ties, slipping on the large rocks that filled the area between them. She fell and cut her hand and jerked it back, shaking off the blood.

She looked at the wound, the rain washing bright red over her hand. Joe yanked his handkerchief out of his pocket, wiped the blood away, and wrapped it around her hand before fresh blood could ooze into her palm. He pushed the base of his hand into hers and wrapped his fingers around her hand. "Keep pressure on it and it should stop bleeding."

Thunder rolled and they hurried down the tracks. As they approached Beef's house Fran saw Ruby sitting on the back porch. Fran yelled above the rain. "Ruby, you ain't seen a little boy come by here, have you?" Ruby didn't answer. "Ruby!" Ruby looked at her. "Where's Beef today?" Ruby sat silent. "Please, Ruby! Where's Beef?"

"Goes to Morristown every Thursday and Friday for work."

Fran pushed the hair off her face and yelled up the embankment again. "A little boy is lost. You seen him?"

Ruby didn't answer but looked up toward the hillside on the opposite side of the tracks. Fran and Joe followed her gaze. They walked farther down the tracks and crossed over the pasture, making their way up the hillside when Joe stopped, pointing. Milo was sitting beneath a giant oak tree, his knees pulled up to his chin, on the other side of the creek. Fred Dog lay beside him, sleeping, despite the rain. Fran sighed and bent over, leaning on her knees. She and Joe walked down the hillside, jumped onto rocks in the creek, and crossed over the water at the shallow end. They walked behind Milo and Fran fell to the ground beside him, exhausted and soaked through. Fred bounced up and pushed his nose under her hand. Milo didn't move.

"You ain't gonna catch much this way," Joe said. "I ain't never known a fish that'll jump out of the water into your hands." Milo watched the rain hit the creek. "You been here long?"

Milo shook his head. "Just a little bit. Thought this big tree would keep me dry."

Joe watched the rain splash onto Milo's arms and looked up through the limbs. "It's doing a poor job, ain't it?" Milo nodded. "Where you been?"

Milo shrugged. "All over."

"You eat anything?" Fran asked.

"Found me some apples this morning," he said, pulling one from his pocket.

"You got Jane and John scared to death," she said. "You about scared me to death, too. A pregnant woman was scared in Greeneville when somebody jumped out behind a building to hit her over the head and it scared the baby right out of her. That's gonna happen to me if you run off like this again."

Milo picked a soggy buttercup and tore it apart. "I ain't meaning to scare nobody."

"I know," she said. She leaned up and pressed the bloodied handkerchief into her hand. "You just don't know what to do with yourself and, truth is, I don't know what to do, either." Milo picked another buttercup and began to shred it. "If you need to run off every now and then that'll be okay." He glanced up at her. "You just need to tell me so I don't get scared and have the baby right where I'm standing. I wish you wouldn't take a notion to go during a rainstorm, either." Milo was quiet. "Why'd you run off?"

He rolled the apple around in his hands. "The tobacco's in and they ain't nothin' more for me to do."

"So your work's all done and you ain't no use anymore?"

"You gonna send me away to them people in Greeneville. But they ain't wanting me, neither. They just being nice cause I'm colored like them."

Fran and Joe were still, listening to the rain slap the leaves of the tree. The whistle of the evening train blew and they watched as it clanked its way past them. "Forty-six cars," she said. "I've been counting them rail cars as long as I can remember. When I was a little girl I counted a hundred and thirty-eight of them one time. Boy, that was something to see that long train chugging its way past me. I sat right down on the embankment over yonder and counted every single car, and when the caboose blew past me I ran like fire down these tracks so I could run tell my mama that the longest train in my life had just passed. She said we needed to celebrate my seeing the longest train of my life and I helped her make a chocolate cake that was this high. That was the best day." Milo ran his hand over the grass, watching the cows walk across the hill in front of him. "Then late in the evening she fell over and died real sudden. Her heart stopped. In a flash the best day of my life turned into the worst one." She shook her head and looked up into the clouds, letting the rain splash onto her face.

"She died and everything changed. It was all different and never the same again." Milo looked at her. "It wasn't. And there came a time when I finally knew that. Not at first. It took me a good long while before it sunk in that my mama wasn't coming back and nothing would ever be like it was. Somehow I had to get on without my mama in this world and find some sort of normal again. It's the only thing we can do when somebody dies. We just have to get on in whatever way we can." She wiped the rain off her face with both hands.

"Milo, I don't have a whole lot of friends in this world, but I can say that in the short time I knew your mama she was one of the finest friends I ever had." He watched as rain dribbled through the leaves of the tree onto his palm. "When she asked me to take you in I didn't think twice about it because I thought the world of your mama. I told her that I would look after you and I mean to keep that promise. I should have told you about that preacher and his wife. When they came by the house and said they'd take you in, well, I wondered if that might be the right thing to do. I wondered if you'd be better off in the long run with a colored family—if you'd be better off with anybody but me." He looked up at her and she ran her hand down Fred's back. "And my letting you go see them people ain't got nothing to do with me not wanting you. I just want to do what's going to be best for you, and if that means that you decide to live with the Aldens then I need to let you do that. But if you decide you want to stay with us, well, I'm going to do whatever it takes to raise you like your mama wanted."

Milo rolled the apple up and down his leg. "Your mama told me that we always make it through. Somehow we always manage to make it to the other side of something." She wiped the rain off her arms, thinking. "I don't have any idea how we're going to make it through to the other side of this, Milo, but if your mama said we'll make it then I believe we will. But I can't do it by myself. If you decide to stay then I need you to help me, too." He squinted as rain stung his eyes. "I know we don't look like you and you don't look like us but I believe we can be a family. I know it don't feel that way now but it will. Someday."

"How you know?"

"Cause it sure didn't take long for me to feel like your mama was family." Her voice tightened and a flood of emotion filled her throat. "It broke my heart when she died." Tears fell down her face and she brushed them away. Milo leaned in to her and she wrapped her arms around him.

"I want my mama and daddy and Rose."

"I know you do," she said, rocking him back and forth. She held on to him as he cried and squeezed him tight. "You're gonna be all right," she said, close to his ear. "It might take a long while but you'll get through to the other side someday. I promise." She looked up at Joe and he smiled. She recognized that smile from high school and she turned her head before she thought too much about it. When Milo was ready Joe picked him up, letting him rest on his shoulder as they walked home in the rain.

When we climbed into bed that night, Mama came in and pulled the covers up to our necks. She stood there for the longest time just looking at us. She walked over to Milo but he had already turned to face the window. She tucked the covers around him and then rested her hand on his arm. "I'll see you all in the morning." We looked over at Milo's silhouette in the moonlight. There was nothing we could say but there had to be something we could do. I nudged John and he pushed the sheet off himself and got out of bed. He walked over to Milo's bed, slid in next to him, and put his arm around him. I swung my feet to the floor and tiptoed over, sliding in next to John. I wrapped my arm around him, with my hand resting on Milo's shoulder, and fell asleep. We stayed that way till morning.

Chapter
NINE

We were finishing breakfast when Joe pulled into our driveway. Mama walked onto the porch and we followed her. John and Milo and I were quiet, watching as he stepped out of the truck and walked toward us.

"Wanted to say good-bye," he said, kneeling in front of us.

"When you coming back?" I asked, holding back tears.

"Couple of months. When it's time to go to auction."

"The Carter Family's coming. Ain't you gonna come back to hear them sing?"

Joe looked at me and smiled. "That sounds like a good idea." I threw myself on him and hugged his neck. John and Milo wrapped their arms around us. "You all be good." I felt tears burning my eyes and held tighter to him. "You take care of your mama." I nodded and let him go.

He rubbed Milo's head. "I'll see you when I get back." Milo nodded and rubbed his hand under his nose.

Joe stood and looked at Mama. "You take care, Fran."

"You, too, Joe." I wanted to stop everything that was happening. I wanted my mother to ask him to stay in Morgan Hill but I knew she wouldn't. I knew she'd let him walk away, right out of all our lives. She held out her hand and Joe shook it before rubbing John and Milo and me on top of our heads again. We ran after him as he walked to his truck and got behind the wheel. He pulled away and his face looked pained. Tears fell down my cheeks as I waved good-bye.

Henry arrived the next morning to take Milo to the Aldens'. Milo stood to take his breakfast plate to the sink. "We'll get that," Mama said.

Milo set his plate down and looked at her. "Mister Alden said he'd bring you home in time for supper. So you have a real good day with them and we'll see you then."

Milo nodded. John and I sat still, looking at the table. Henry took Milo's hand and walked him to his truck. John and I ran from the kitchen and stood on the porch, watching as they left. Milo turned around and looked at us through the truck window and we both waved, trying to smile.

I turned to go back into the kitchen; Mama was standing behind us. I didn't say anything but walked past her. "He ain't always going to be little, Jane. One day he's going to be grown and he'd want to know if there was colored folk who would have taken him in." I shook my head and moved closer to the door. "He needs to do this," she said. I threw open the door and let it slam behind me. She didn't respond; there was no point in arguing. We'd just have to wait out the day and see what happened.

Milo looked out the passenger window and watched mud fly up past the tires. "What do I do, Mister Henry?"

"You just get to know these people. Ask them anything you want."

"And then what?"

Henry held on to the wheel and shifted in his seat. "Someday you're gonna be great big like your daddy, and you're gonna look around at the faces at the supper table and all them faces gonna be black or some of them will be white. That'll be up to you."

Milo held on to the door handle as the truck turned onto another road fresh with potholes. "How I gonna know who to pick?"

"I ain't got no idea," Henry said. "All I know is whenever I need to think about something real hard, I go off to a special place and do some real good thinking." Milo was quiet. Henry reached over and put a hand on the back of his head. "That probably don't help you too much, but you weren't brought through that fire to be left alone now." Milo stared out the window for the rest of the drive.

John and I finished work at the house and then headed to the store. I was still fuming inside and didn't notice Alvin Dodson. He hadn't rubbed cockleburs in my hair since my daddy died, and I hadn't seen him since Mama and Milo walked down the tracks with us. He was hiding behind a thick magnolia tree, armed with a handful of cockleburs; but I wasn't in the mood for Alvin that morning. He jumped onto the tracks in front of us. "Hey, Jaaaaane," he said. He laughed and I felt blood rush to my head. I spun my arms 'round and 'round like a windmill and hit him with my dinner bucket. I heard the bucket catch him on the head and then saw a small trickle of blood creep down his forehead but I didn't stop flailing. "Ow," he yelled, bringing the hand full of cockleburs up to cover his head. I pounced on him and rubbed his own grubby handful of cockleburs into his ratty hair. "Ow!" he screamed louder, trying to push me off.

I stood up and grabbed my dinner bucket, yelling in his ear. "I've had it with you and your low-down meanness, Alvin Dodson." John stood on top of the rail and I grabbed his hand, yanking him down onto the tracks. "You stay away from us from now on." Alvin sat on the tracks crying, trying to pull the cockleburs out of his hair.

"She got into another fight," John said as we entered the store. I tried to hush him but it was too late. He gave a blow-by-blow account for Mama and Loretta.

"What in the world is wrong with you?" Mama asked. I ignored her and walked outside.

When he got back from Greeneville Henry unloaded chicken feed from the back of his truck and stacked it on the porch. "You plan on giving your mama the silent treatment all day?" I shrugged and dragged a bag of feed from the back of his truck and up the steps. "There was a man in Johnson City who never smiled." He stopped his work and placed his finger on my forehead. "He held his brows the way yours have looked today. All bunched up together like that. Well, don't you know that his face froze, and now whenever he sees people they all think he's mad at them so he ain't got nary a friend in this world." I lifted my brows and opened my mouth wide, sliding my jaw from side to side. Henry threw the last two bags on the stack and sat on the porch steps.

I plopped down next to him. "What were them colored folk like?"

"They're real nice people. They got a boy who's still at home. He's older, about fifteen or so, but he's a real good boy. I could tell."

I looked down and watched an ant crawl over my big toe and disappear. It popped back up and headed over the next toe. I wriggled my foot and it fell to the ground. "You reckon he's better off with them people because they're colored?"

"That might mean something, Pretty Girl. It sure might."

Somehow in my heart I knew that Milo would be better off with the Aldens but I didn't want to hear it. I looked for the ant and saw it make its way back up the step. "So he'll go with them, won't he?"

"I don't know."

"If he was your boy would you want Milo to live with them?"

"I'd want my boy to live with a family where he would be loved and taken care of."

I lifted my head and looked at him. "Could the Aldens do that?"

"Yes. But so could you all."

"But the Aldens are a normal family. We ain't never been much of a family, Henry."

"No such thing as normal," he said. He stood and brushed off his pants. "Milo has a hard decision in front of him. And I know you don't want to hear this but your mama did what was right." I looked up at him and scowled. "Now be careful because your face will freeze like that." He went inside the store and left me alone on the steps where I waited the rest of the day for Milo.

I tried to come up with reasons to hate the Aldens and hoped that they would be obvious to Milo during his visit, but when they arrived with him that afternoon I realized they had given him no reason to dislike them. As they sat on the store porch my heart fell because I knew they were good people.

We didn't talk about Milo's visit with the Aldens around Mama. We waited till we went to bed that night and I sat on the edge of Milo's bed. John had already determined he would sleep with Milo from now on, so I pushed him over to make room for me. "Was they nice?" I asked. Milo lay with his hands behind his head and nodded. "Was their boy nice?"

He nodded again. "He's got a baseball and we threw it in the street."

I sighed. We didn't have a baseball. "Was their house big?"

"Nope. Little. They let me see the room I'd sleep in where the big kids used to sleep."

I put my hands around my ankles and rested my chin on top of my knee. At our house he'd have to share the bedroom with John and me. "When they coming back?"

"Few days I guess. That's when I'll go with them or stay here." He leaned up on his elbows, looking at me. "What you reckon I should do?"

"We want you to stay here," John said.

I rolled my chin around the top of my knee, thinking. "We do. But we ain't never had a baseball or a street to throw it in."

"We got a genuine pilot's cap, though," John said.

"I guess we could get a baseball somewhere if

need be." I looked out the window and saw Fred on the porch making his bed for the night. I didn't want to say what I was thinking. "But they got them a good daddy in that house and we ain't. We ain't never had a good daddy and we can't get one of them somewhere. We only got Mama." There wasn't anything else to say, so I checked under their bed for the bogeyman and then lay down on my bed.

John grabbed Milo's hand and held on to it as he fell asleep, but Milo and I stayed awake till late in the night, thinking.

I placed a bucket under Flo and dragged a stool next to her. I pulled on her teats and she turned her head; she was chewing a massive cud. I couldn't see Milo but I heard him talking with John. "What do you do in school?" My heart jumped at the thought of school.

"Set there and listen to the teacher yap all day," John said.

"That don't sound no good at all."

"It ain't a bit of good but they make ya go so they can learn you how to read and cipher and name all the daggum states."

I tried to peer under Flo's great belly. "It ain't nothing like that, John." Flo picked up her foot and set it inside the milk bucket. I hollered and smacked her backside, punching at her leg till she lifted it clear. "School helps you not be ignorant anymore so you can be somebody when you grow up."

"Is it scary?" Milo asked.

I smacked Flo's backside again to keep her from moving and pulled faster on her teats. "It ain't none bit scary."

"It might be scary in Greeneville," he said.

I thought for a moment. "Well, it probably is scary in Greeneville because people will knock you over the head, but here in Morgan Hill it ain't. Mister Jeffers is the principal and about the finest man you'll ever meet. And the teachers are fine, too. All of them except Old Lady Griggs. Kids put snakes and bugs in her desk but she don't appreciate them and is just as mean as she can be. But them other teachers are real good and they'll teach you reading and writing like nobody's business." Milo worked at filling his bucket and didn't ask any more questions but I was shaking inside. It seemed we were facing a mountain every time we turned around.

That night I sat on the side of Mama's bed. She looked up at me. "School's starting in two days." She nodded. "Is he going to Greeneville?"

She sighed. "I don't know, Jane. That depends on if he lives with the Aldens."

"But if he lived here he still ain't allowed to go with us?" She shook her head. My legs were shaking but I stood to my feet. "Then I ain't going, neither." I waited for her to tell me that in no uncertain terms I would indeed go to school, but she didn't say anything, so I walked to my room and went to bed wondering what in the world I had done.

Farmers needed plenty of time to bring in their crops so school started the Thursday after Labor Day that year. When I told John that I wasn't going to school because Milo wasn't allowed to go, he whooped and hollered and carried on like Santa himself had visited. He planted his feet and said, "Well, if you and Milo ain't going then I ain't going, neither." He tried to pretend that he was being noble and brave but I knew better.

Mama walked with us to the store and I saw classmates making their way over the roads and through the fields. I felt sick. I loved school and wanted to be there. I stood on the porch of the store and could see Mr. Jeffers greeting each student as they climbed the steps. I tried to help Henry put cash in the register but my heart wasn't in it. "Can I go over there and say hey to my friends?" Mama nodded and I ran as fast as I could up the hill but I was too late; everyone was already inside.

I sat on the steps and waited for anyone else who might be running late. "Come on, Jane, the school bell rang." I turned around and saw Delores Cockburn standing at the top of the stairs.

"I ain't going to school, Miz Cockburn."

"Are you sick?"

"No. Since Milo can't go to school then me and John ain't going, neither."

Delores arched her brows and walked back inside. The scowl on her face told me I had put her right in the middle of some kind of dilemma. I wondered again what I had done but had no time to think; within minutes Bill Jeffers was at my side. "Jane, what on earth are you doing out here?"

"Me and John ain't able to go to school this year."

He was quiet as he looked down the hill to the store. "Why aren't you coming to school?"

"If Milo ain't able to go then we ain't able to, either."

"Milo's a colored boy."

"I'm colored, too. I'm colored white. So I can't go, neither."

"Jane, does your mama know that you aren't in school today?" I nodded. "And she's okay with this?"

I shrugged. "I reckon she knows that if she made us go we'd just walk through them doors when she was watching and then walk right back out 'em when she wasn't. Reckon she knows we're just as stubborn as she is."

He walked back inside but I felt him watching me from the front doors. I sat motionless. I understood then that my sitting there and staying out of school had created a predicament for Bill. I wasn't fully aware of what was happening but I was determined to stay put.

"What is she doing?" Fran asked, pacing. "John, run up there and tell Jane to come on back now."

"Hold on, Fran," Henry said. "Let her come back when she's ready."

"But what is she doing?"

"Let's just see."

I stayed on the step till dinnertime, singing and telling the story of the Three Musketeers to myself. When the school doors opened I was bombarded with questions. Miss Harmon reached me first. "Jane Gable, why aren't you in school today?" Twenty people must have asked me that in the next five minutes. Several students ran to the store for dinner and I could only imagine what they were talking about with Henry, Loretta, and

Mama. Louise Hankins sat next to me and ate her dinner, but when it was time to go back inside she stayed with me. She didn't say anything. She just smiled and rested her chin on her knees. My body was hot with shame because of all the times I avoided her on our walk to school. Of all the people to sit with me! I believe she sat there because she didn't feel like she fit into the school any more than Milo would if he were allowed. J. R. Cass walked up the hill from Henry's and sat next to us as well. J. R. was the last of sixteen children of the poorest family in Morgan Hill.

John brought my dinner and threw up his hands. "What in tarnation are you doing, Jane?"

"I want to go to school so I'm going to sit here till Milo can go with us."

"Me, too," Louise said. J. R. shrugged and smiled.

Defeated, John shook his head and sat down.

Henry watched through the store window and laughed. "Looks like we got us a revolution of sorts!"

Fran wrung her hands and pretended to busy herself. "She's going to cause all sorts of trouble." She stepped toward the door and Henry stopped her.

"They're just sitting, Fran. Far as I know sitting ain't against the law around here."

"What are they doing just sitting there?" Milo asked.

Henry knelt down next to him. "They're telling people something."

"But they ain't saying nothin'."

Henry looked up the hill and smiled. "Sometimes that's the best way to say anything."

Teachers came to talk to us throughout the afternoon and I always knew when Mr. Jeffers was standing at the front doors watching us. When the dismissal bell rang we all walked to the store and went home.

On Friday morning Milo walked to the store with Mama, and John and I climbed the hill to the school and sat on the same step as we had the day before. Louise and J.R. arrived and took their places beside us. When loudmouth Delroy Jenks knew why we were sitting there he sat down, too. I don't think Delroy was making any sort of statement other than that he wanted to get out of school, but we appreciated the extra body. We knew the teachers were talking with Mr. Jeffers about us but we pretended not to hear.

• • •

"How long they all gonna sit there?" Milo asked.

"Till something happens," Henry said.

"What are they wanting to happen?"

Henry looked down at him and smiled. "They're wanting something to change."

"Did I bring that trouble on, Mister Henry?"

"No, Milo. You ain't done one thing wrong. It's been a long time coming."

At mid-morning Otis and Nona Dodd walked up the steps of the school. Nona had fried chicken and lots of potato salad for us. Before he ran groceries Henry brought an Orange Crush and Moon Pies for everybody and promised to be back in the afternoon with ice cream sandwiches. By then Del and Helen Cannon had joined us, along with Jeb Hancock and Ray and Olive Harper. Loretta showed up still wearing her apron from the store.

Before dinner Beef stormed through the door at Henry's. A handful of people were with him. Fran was at the register finishing with a customer. She hadn't seen Beef since he, Dewey, and Clyde came to her house. "What are you doing, Fran?" he asked. She pulled Milo to her side. "That little nigger boy ain't got no right in that school." When he heard Beef's voice Henry walked out of the stockroom and stood next to Fran. "We all know what you're trying to do."

Her face turned crimson and she felt sweat break out on her back. "I ain't doing a thing, Beef, and this little boy has every right to go to school."

Henry looked at the faces of the people with Beef and frowned. "Beef," he said, "it seems you of all people would want to see him get educated."

Beef pointed to the schoolhouse. "That ain't right, Henry. Niggers go to their own schools and you know that. We all know it."

Voices rose behind Beef, and now Fran felt the sweat drip down her back and chest. Henry threw up his hands and shouted above the noise. "Did we win the war only to lose the battle here?" Beef stared at him. Henry walked to the door and opened it. "You all need to get on home." No one moved. "Fran, pick up the phone and call Sheriff Dutton and tell him I got trespassers." She picked up the phone and began to dial.

A few shuffled toward the door; no one looked at Fran as they left. Beef stuck a stubby finger in Henry's face. "You know we can do something about this, Henry."

Henry shrugged and held the door wider for him.

❖ ❖ ❖

Beef's truck rumbled up the driveway and stopped in front of the steps. He yanked Louise up by the arm. I stood and watched as he dragged her to the truck, throwing her in the passenger side. She stared at me through the open window and her lips formed a tiny smile. She hung out the window and looked at me as Beef sped down the driveway and out onto the road.

At dinnertime the steps were swarming with kids. By then they all knew what we were doing and were eager to get a look at us. Bill Jeffers paced at the top of the stairs with his hand over his mouth but I swear I saw him smiling.

That afternoon Pete and Charlotte Fletcher arrived with half of the Morgan Hill Baptist Church (the other half firmly believing that Milo needed to go to a colored school). The adults entered the school and in the next several minutes they walked out the front doors with their children. Henry honked as he pulled into the drive of the school and everyone clapped when he stood on the bed of his truck and threw ice cream sandwiches into the small crowd.

We could see many of the teachers and Bill Jeffers inside the school building, pressing their noses to the windows to count the heads on the stairs.

They didn't know what to do anymore because half their students were spread across the steps.

At the end of the day Bill Jeffers snuck through the back doors of the school and made his way to the store. Milo was with Henry so Fran was alone when Bill arrived. "Afternoon, Fran."

She was surprised to see him. "Hi, Bill. Anything new?"

He laughed and shuffled his feet. "No, not a thing in this world." Fran handed change to her customer and looked at Bill. "Fran, one day I'm going to leave this world and people will talk about me. When they do I don't want any of them to say, 'He was the one who kept that little colored boy out of school.'"

She felt her heart jump. "What about the rules?"

"Sometimes rules are wrong."

"Will you get in trouble?"

"It won't be the first time and I've always held my own pretty good when it comes to an argument. Besides, I've written down every single name that's out on those steps, so if I need anybody to back me up I know exactly who to call!"

"What about Delores?"

"Don't worry about Delores."

"What about the teachers?"

"They're at that school to teach. That's what we're all there for so that's what we're going to do."

"There's a lot of folks who won't like it. They were in here this morning."

"I know. They came to the school. We'll just have to cross each bridge when we come to it. It won't be easy, Fran. Guess if we all know that going in, we'll know what we're in for."

She couldn't feel her legs. She walked Bill to the door and leaned against the rail of the porch; her heart was pounding. It was a hot afternoon, the kind Addy had always liked, when the air was thick and lay heavy on her skin.

She watched Bill walk the hill to the school and he shouted something to the crowd. She heard a soft roar as everyone cheered. She laughed and squinted into the sky. "We just got our first cup of cold water, Addy."

Chapter
TEN

"Milo," Mama said at supper that evening. "The Aldens called me today at the store." He looked at her; his eyes were big as saucers. "Have you been studying on where you want to live?" He nodded.

"We want him to live here, Mama," John said.

She cut her eyes at him and John quieted down. "We'd love for you to stay but that might not be what's best for you." I moved the eggs around on my plate and wished she'd stop talking. "School's started here and in Greeneville and

I'll need to call them. Do you understand what I'm saying?" He nodded and pushed his plate away. I pushed mine away, too. I couldn't eat.

After the Pet Milk Company picked up our milk cans the next morning Milo ran back to the house. I found him rummaging through the ice-box. "What're ya looking for?"

"Where's them biscuits and sausages from breakfast?"

I opened the door of the oven and took out a bowl covered with a plate. "You still hungry?"

"I might be later," he said, wrapping all the biscuits and sausages in a dish towel.

"What're you doing?"

"I need to find me a place for thinking."

"Where you going *now*?" I asked.

I hadn't climbed the hills leading to Widow's Mountain in years. The last time I'd been that far was three winters earlier. John and I had trudged up the blanket of snow covering the hillsides with Pete, Charlotte, and two of their four children, each of us holding a side of an old truck fender that Pete had hammered into a sled. Three of us would sit on the sled and plunge head first down the hillside, screaming till we reached bottom. We didn't slide down Widow's Mountain.

Even though it wasn't really a mountain it was still too big for a makeshift sled and much too big to climb.

"What you planning on doing when we get there?" I asked Milo.

"I plan on going right to the top of it to do me some thinking."

I stopped in my tracks. "You can't climb Widow's Mountain. Ain't nobody can. It's rock straight up." But Milo wasn't listening. He ran up the hillsides and John and I followed close behind. We sunk into the wet ground with each step we took, so we rolled up the legs of our overalls and the mud and water splattered drippy, dark streaks on our shins and calves.

We reached the mountain and gawked straight up the rock at the base of it. "We can't get up that," I said.

"Well, I'm going up it," Milo said, stuffing the towel full of biscuits into the front of his overalls.

"That rock is slick as can be. We can't climb it."

Milo ran around the base looking for something and John followed. "That's the place. We can wedge right in there," he said, pointing to a crevice that attached Widow's Mountain to the hill next to it.

"We can't shimmy up in there! We'll get stuck

and won't nobody hear us screaming. We'll die sure enough. And John can't do it on account of that gimp arm."

John tossed the sling on the ground. "I don't need this," he said, fastening the pilot's cap beneath his chin. He stood with his hands on his hips and sized up the height to the crevice. He cupped his hands and offered them to Milo. Milo stepped into them but John couldn't lift him high enough to grasp inside the cleft. Milo fell to the ground. John sighed and looked at me. "Jane, come on! My arm still hurts too much to lift him by myself." I threw my hands in the air and marched over to help. John and I locked our fingers together and formed a step for Milo's feet. We lifted him higher and higher until he placed one foot on my shoulder and the other against the opening. I cringed under the weight and felt Milo wobble. I grabbed his leg and held him steady as he reached for a rock jutting out inside the crevice.

"I got it!" he said, wedging himself into the space. He straddled his legs on each side of the split and grinned. "That ain't nothing but easy!" I shook my head and moaned. John was too short to get inside the crevice by himself.

I knelt down on one knee and pointed to my shoulders. "Come on! Hurry up. Mama will fly all over us when she finds out we ain't home picking the last of them beans." John straddled my shoulders and I balanced myself as I stood under the weight.

"Closer," John said, digging his heels into my sides. "Closer." I heard him groan as he reached for something to grab on to but he couldn't. "Higher, Jane." I slid my hands between my shoulders and his thighs and strained to push him up. "Got it," he said. His foot settled onto my head and he steadied himself as he wriggled inside the gap. He pushed himself off my head and I fell to the ground, exhausted. He groaned as he wormed his way through the crevice.

"Don't hurt your blamed arm again," I yelled.

"Come on, Jane," Milo said, pulling himself out of the crack and stepping onto the rock that jutted out at the top. "There ain't nothing to it."

I stretched my arms over my head in the grass. "I can't do it. I'm pooped."

"We all gotta go or ain't none of us going," Milo said.

John crawled onto the rock and hung his legs over the side. "Don't be yella, Jane."

"I ain't yella!"

"You look yella to me."

I jumped to my feet. "I'm gonna box your ears."

"You gonna have to get up here first," he said, swinging his legs.

I put my foot on a rock at the base of the hill and then hoisted my other foot into the side of the wedge. I pushed myself up and placed a foot against another rock as I reached over my head. I put my hand inside a shaft and then was on my way, stepping and pulling myself up toward the top. I reached for a rock and a jagged stone ripped the flesh on my arm. "I cut my doggone arm," I yelled. I dug my elbows into the sides of the crevice and moaned as I pushed myself closer to the opening. I pulled myself out of the top of the crevice and John and Milo sat in front of me, smiling. "That wasn't easy," I said, looking over my scrapes and wounds. John and Milo raised each of their arms in front of me and grinned, proud of the nicks and bruises and blood-streaked skin they'd received on their way up.

At mid-morning Fran returned to the store from running groceries and threw the truck keys on the counter, waving a note in the air. "Them youngins have run off to Widow's Mountain."

Henry lifted his head out of the cooler. "What?"

"Went home to see how they were coming along in the garden. They ain't nowhere to be found but they left this." She wadded the note and put her fist on her hip. "They've never gone off to Widow's Mountain before. What in the world has gotten into them?"

Loretta stopped sweeping. "Henry Walker, why do I think you've got something to do with this?"

Henry closed the door to the cooler. "I beg your pardon, Missus Walker, but I've been at this store since seven o'clock this morning. How could I have anything to do with this?" Loretta kept staring. "And I resent the accusing tone in your eyes but I do accept your apology."

"What is wrong with them?" Fran asked. "They know better than to leave like this."

"I'll head out and bring 'em home," Henry said.

"You ain't got no business climbing up and down them hillsides, Henry," Loretta said. "You're getting too old."

He pretended to be too deaf to hear and the door clanged shut behind him.

"Well, we got up the crevice so let's get back home before Mama finds out we ain't there," I said.

Milo looked at the top of the hill and began to climb. "I already told ya. I'm going up this here mountain to do me some thinking."

John followed and again I threw my hands in the air. "Come back here, John."

"I got me some thinking to do, too," he said.

I watched as they raced toward the top of the hill then ran after them. They heard me running behind them and tried to outrun me. I grabbed Milo around the waist and swung him to the ground. He shrieked with laughter. I slipped and stumbled up the hillside, the boys screaming behind me. After several minutes we fell onto the grass out of breath. I sat up and looked at the town.

"Look at that," I said. "It sure is something from up here."

Milo pointed to the top. "Wait till we see it from up there." He stood to his feet and started toward the top again.

I wasn't good at judging time but figured it must have taken us over an hour to reach the top. When we did Milo raised his hands in the air. John and I stood at either side of him and we could see in every direction. It was breathtaking. For as long as I'd been alive I'd seen such a small corner of Morgan Hill but now it was all right there, beautiful and rolling green as far as I could see.

"There's our house," John said. "And the Cannons'."

"There's Henry's," I said. "And the school and the church." We kept pointing and naming houses and farms and I noticed Milo had grown quiet. I turned around and saw him sitting with his knees pulled up under his chin. I sat down beside him. "You doing your thinking?"

He nodded. John sat down and pulled his knees up under his chin. We sat in the quiet and felt the breeze on our faces as we watched the cattle graze in the pastures below. "What's he doing?" John asked, leaning in to me.

"He's thinking."

" 'Bout what?"

I shrugged. We sat in silence and soaked in the view as Milo did his thinking, gazing out over the pastures and hillsides as if he was looking for something. I followed his eyes and we watched as the train barreled its way through Morgan Hill. It looked so small from where we were sitting. The whistle blew and I put my chin on my knees. Milo pulled the towel full of sausage biscuits out of his overalls, handing one each to John and me. The three of us ate in silence.

"I wonder if them Three Musketeers would help your mama if they lived here?"

I stopped eating and looked at him. "I reckon they would. But they're just folks in a story."

"I been studying on what you said about not

having a daddy." Milo filled his mouth with the last of the sausage biscuit. "Since you ain't got no daddy, seems your mama needs folk like the Three Musketeers to help her."

"Them fellas are in a storybook," I said. "They ain't real, no how."

"They's three of us," Milo said. "I been thinkin' we could stick together like them Three Musketeers."

I didn't have time to respond; a figure was walking over the hillsides toward us. "Who is that?" I asked. Milo and John got up. I put my hand over my eyes. "It's Henry," I yelled. "I bet Mama's fit to be tied and sent him after us!" I reached for John's and Milo's hands and the three of us ran down the side of the hill, slipping and falling as we went. I felt my heart racing and ran faster, hoping and praying that somehow Henry found our note and not Mama. John laughed as we tumbled down and it made me mad. "It ain't gonna be so funny when Mama knocks us into next week," I said.

Milo giggled as I fell on my backside and began to slide; he did the same, bumping and groaning as he tumbled. He stopped running and a broad smile covered his face. He pretended to raise a sword. "I'm Porthos!"

John pulled an imaginary sword from his side.

"And I'm Aramis!" They bobbed and weaved and ducked beneath the blades of their swords as they chased each other down the hillside.

Not to be outdone I ran after them and screamed, "I'm Athos!" for all of Morgan Hill to hear. I forgot about Mama's anger for a moment and we yelled and laughed the rest of the way down the side of that hill. We reached the bottom and stopped to catch our breath, looking over the flat rock edge.

Henry was at the base of the mountain, looking up at us. "So the Three Musketeers have been getting into all sorts of trouble this morning, huh?" He'd heard everything.

We smiled and gasped for breath. "All for one," John yelled, raising his sword in the air.

"And one for all," Milo and I said, raising our swords to the sky.

We inched our way back through the crevice and Henry helped each of us to the ground, checking our scrapes and bruises. "Well, what in the world are you three doing going up Widow's Mountain?"

"Milo had to do some thinking," I said.

"Is that so? Did you get your thinking done, Milo?" Milo nodded. "Could you see all of Morgan Hill up there?" He nodded again.

"And what'd you think?"

"I think it looks mighty nice," Milo said. Henry smiled and pulled Milo in to his side.

Mama called the Aldens from the store and told them Milo had made his decision. They promised to stay in touch and they did. We saw them often throughout the years. I have only vague recollections about the rest of that day, but I vividly recall the feeling of relief when Milo's decision soaked in and I realized he would make his home with us. We didn't know what that decision really meant. We were too young and had visions of grand courage and chivalry in our heads. Somehow we thought that if we all just stuck together we'd make it through. When I think about it now I know we were naïve but Henry always called it bravery. Maybe he's right. I can still hear our laughter as we tumbled down that hillside and feel Henry's arms around me as he helped me through the crevice, but my clearest memory is of walking home from the store with Mama on our first journey together as a family. We were going home.

Mama tucked us into bed that night and after she pulled the sheet up over my chest she leaned down and kissed my forehead. I couldn't remember the last time she'd kissed me, and I lay with a startled look on my face. I pulled the sheet under my chin and waved at her with the four fingers that were resting on top of it. She moved to John and Milo's bed and kissed them, too. I smiled when I heard them giggle.

When Mama closed the door Milo sat up in his bed. "What do you reckon it makes me living here?"

"What do you mean?" I asked.

"What am I now?"

I thought for a moment. "You're our brother. What else would you be?" He nodded and lay down. I realized I had forgotten to look under John and Milo's bed for the bogeyman and sprang to their bedside.

John grabbed my arm. "You don't have to do that. I know there ain't nothing there." Maybe he wasn't afraid because he knew it wasn't just me and him but three of us (soon to be four) who would be sticking together this time. I helped them through their prayers and then lay down in my bed and turned to look over at them. I knelt on my knees in my bed and looked out the window into the sky. *Them boys need a daddy,* I prayed. I realized what I was doing and folded my hands. *They need a daddy to help them get along in the world. Please bring us somebody to help Mama take care of us. You know I ain't ever asked for much but we need this real bad.*

• • •

Fran jumped awake and leaned up in her bed. "Who's there?"

"It's me." Milo was standing in the hallway.

"Come on in here. Are you sick?"

"No, ma'am."

"Then what are you doing out of bed?"

"Them youngins ain't gonna like me being at school."

She sat up so she could see him in the moonlight. "Well, the truth is, some of them won't but a lot of them will. And some of them won't like you as a friend but you won't like some of them, either. That's just how it is." She leaned in closer. "But you'll find a lot of youngins you do like and they'll like you back so there ain't a thing to worry about."

"None of them look like me."

"But if we all looked the same we wouldn't know if we was coming or going cause we'd be running into ourselves."

"Is it hard?"

She nodded. "Sometimes. But it ain't harder than climbing up Widow's Mountain." She could see him smile.

"Will you come with me?"

"No, I've already been through school, but

Jane and John will be there and you'll learn how to write and read books."

"My mama and daddy didn't know how to read."

"But I know they would have given anything if you could learn."

"Will they know I'm going to school?"

"Yes. And they'll be proud as can be that day."

"Does that man Beef scare you?"

She could see his eyes in the moonlight. "Does he scare you?" He nodded. "Well, you know what? We've got about a million angels surrounding our house."

"Where they at?"

"They're everywhere. And they'll make sure you make it to school safe and sound."

He shuffled away and stood in the doorway. "Night, ma'am," he said, leaving her alone in the darkness.

"Milo!" He stepped back into the room. "Why'd you decide to stay?"

"Cause I need somebody to take care of me and seems you need somebody to take care of you."

She heard him wander through the hallway. She leaned against the headboard and looked out the window. "Help me do this," she whispered.

"Help me, please." She put a hand over her mouth and let the tears fall onto her swollen belly.

The next morning we grabbed our dinner buckets Mama had packed for school and walked out onto the porch. We were startled to see Del and Helen Cannon pull into the driveway followed by Pete and Charlotte Fletcher. Otis and Nona Dodd drove in behind them and then that snake Alvin Dodson's parents, Cal and Viola Dodson. "Well, look at this," Mama said, watching them step out onto the gravel.

"Are them the angels you told me about?" Milo asked.

Mama nodded. "I believe they might be."

Del and Helen walked to us and smiled. "We just wanted to see the youngins get off to school, Fran," Del said, wrapping his arm around Milo's shoulder. Mama smiled and put a hand over her mouth.

"We'll take them in the truck," Helen said.

"No, they can walk straight down the tracks like they always do."

Mama walked us to the embankment and she cupped Milo's chin in her hand. "You have a real good day."

We made our way down the embankment and

hadn't made it to Beef's house when we heard the faint sound of voices. We turned to see Pete and Charlotte and Del and Helen walking behind us, Helen using her cane to steady each step. I looked up at Beef's house and Ruby smiled, lifting her hand in a small wave. Otis and Nona Dodd rode with Cal and Viola Dodson to their house and they stood at the embankment and watched as we walked past them. Cal kept his hand on Alvin's shoulder and Alvin stared sourly as we passed. Olive Harper pretended to pick honeysuckles as we passed the back of her house and she threw her hand up as if saluting. I'd never seen so many people along the tracks. It was as if we were walking along a parade route and we were the main attraction.

John and I held on to Milo's hand as we climbed the steps to the Langley School Building. We didn't know it but Mama, Henry, and Loretta were craning their necks to watch us from a window at the store. Most of the students had never seen Milo and they stopped to look at him as we passed. Louise wasn't there. That no-account Beef kept her home so she wouldn't go to school with a colored boy.

Bill Jeffers stood at the top of the steps and shook Milo's hand. "We sure are happy to have you with us this year, Milo," he said, loud enough for the students to hear. "Let me show you your classroom." They walked to Jeanette Abbott's room. I had had Miss Abbott when I was in first grade and she had been my favorite teacher. She took Milo's hand and led him to the small wooden desk with a bright yellow construction paper sign that said "MILO" in capital letters. She had even put together a box that had two pencils and an eraser in it. "I need a special helper today to help me pass out papers and things. Do you think you could help me do that?" Milo nodded. He was going to have a fine day with Miss Abbott.

At dinnertime John and I planned to walk down the hill to Henry's store with Milo. The front doors of the school were open; Miss Abbott's class was sitting on the front steps eating. Miss Abbott was helping a student with a bloody nose but I didn't see Milo. A group of older boys were huddled around the massive oak tree that stood in the back of the school. I grabbed John's hand and ran toward them.

"Where'd you come from?" I heard one of the boys ask.

"What happened to your mama and daddy?" another asked.

I pushed my way through the middle of them

and discovered Milo pressed against the trunk of the tree. I jumped in front of him and pushed an older boy away. "You all leave him alone!"

"We're just talking."

"He ain't got nothing to say. You got something to ask him you ask me."

One of the boys shoved my shoulder. "Get on away, Jane. We're just asking him stuff."

I rammed both my hands into the boy's chest and heaved with all my might. "Leave him be!" John jumped up and grabbed the boy's arm, pulling him away from me. Another boy wrapped his arms around John's waist and threw him to the ground. "Leave him alone," I said. Another boy yanked my hair and pushed me to the ground, making me scream.

"Leave 'em alone!" I didn't recognize that voice. The boys started to scatter as someone shoved them from behind. "Get out of the way." I looked up and saw Alvin Dodson push the older boys to the side.

"We ain't doing nothing but talking to him," one of the boys said again.

"He'll talk when he's good and ready. Go on and eat your dinner before I run get Mister Jeffers after you." The boys picked up their dinner buckets and sacks and left us alone. Alvin walked back toward the school. I watched him move away and then he turned and smiled at me. Things sure were changing in Morgan Hill.

I ran screaming down the hill to Henry's with John and Milo. We didn't know that we were racing headlong into the dead of winter—and none of us was ready.

Chapter
ELEVEN

Fall and winter was always exciting for me because the Carter Family came each year to sing and Loretta directed the Christmas pageant at the church. For three years running I played the role of Mary. By the end of each summer I was already looking forward to rehearsals.

The Carter Family was coming to Morgan Hill on the first Saturday of December and I couldn't wait because Joe said he'd come back for it. When that night arrived the gymnasium in the schoolhouse bustled with people from the surrounding communities who brought baskets full of fried chicken, biscuits, green beans, mashed potatoes, and every dessert possible. The room filled with pipe and cigarette smoke and the aroma of chicken and ham. Women wore their best cotton dresses and men left their caps at home. Henry splashed on cologne and Mama and Loretta wouldn't let him hear the end of it.

"What's that called?" Loretta asked.

"It said Garden Surprise on the bottle."

Mama and Loretta held on to each other and laughed. Poor Henry. He could never get a break.

When Joe walked through the front door John and Milo and I ran and jumped on him, knocking him down. Mama watched from across the gymnasium and I swear I saw her smile.

We ate throughout the night and Mama, Loretta, Helen, and other women busied themselves putting out a fresh bowl of green beans or another basket of rolls or a fresh pie. Clyde and Dewey were there but they stayed outside for the most part drinking on the tailgate of Dewey's truck. The Carter Family sang and a lot of people stomped and kicked their heels in the middle of the gymnasium floor. Earlier in the day men had laid a large, flat piece of wood on the floor and covered it with sawdust. I grabbed John's and Milo's hands and we spun and swung our legs and danced till we fell down in exhaustion. I watched Joe and wished he'd ask my mother to dance but I knew it wouldn't do any good; she didn't dance and I knew she wouldn't start now. I stood on top of Henry's feet and he danced me around the room, knocking over three people in the process.

I went with Joe to eat a piece of pie. "Can I have two pieces, Mama?"

"Why not?" she said, putting pieces of butterscotch and lemon in front of me.

Joe picked up a piece and began to eat it. "You look real nice, Fran."

"Thank you, Joe. How long you staying?"

"Don't rightly know."

"Well, it's good to have you home."

Joe looked at the floor and took another bite of pie. "This is real good."

"Charlotte made it."

"I'll need to tell Charlotte it's real good." I rolled my eyes. They were hopeless.

I never wanted that night to end. Milo jumped around and laughed so much that, for the first time, the memory of the fire wasn't the first thing I thought of when I looked at him. It's funny what can be called to mind when you look back on things. I can't recall a word the Carter Family sang but I remember the sound of their guitars, mandolins, and bass in the background as I danced and ate and ran through that smoky gymnasium. I can hear the sawdust crunching beneath my feet and see Henry's face as he twirled me around the floor, and I remember glimpses of Mama running for another pie or cake. And in a drawn-out moment I can see myself running when I spotted her hanging limp in Joe's arms as he carried her out of the building.

Fran and Loretta had worked throughout the night keeping food on the tables. Late in the evening when Fran reached for a blackberry pie it slipped out of her hands and fell, dark liquid and berries spreading over the floor where the women were working. She scooped up the gloppy mess and threw it back into the pie tin. Loretta handed her a towel. "No," Fran said. "That's somebody's good towel. Let me get some rags."

The hallway was dark behind the gymnasium but Fran walked to the janitor's closet and fumbled for the light string dangling from the ceiling. She pulled on it and looked for a bin or crate of rags. She spotted a bucket on the bottom shelf and bent to grab a handful of rags.

"You look awful pretty tonight, Fran."

She screamed and jumped. "Dewey! What on earth are you doing back here?"

"I seen you needed help."

She smelled liquor and forced a ghost of a smile. "I just needed some old rags." She walked toward the door but he blocked it. "I got me a mess to clean up."

"Loretta can take care of that mess. Just stay here and talk. We could pick up where we left off that day at your house."

The reckless look on his face frightened her and she stepped back. "This old janitor's closet ain't no place to talk. The gymnasium's the place for that. It's got all that good food." She tried to move past again but Dewey filled the doorway.

"You know I didn't come to your house all them nights just because I liked playing cards with Lonnie." His face was close and she shrank back. He pressed his mouth onto hers and she turned her head, frightened at his touch. "God, you are some woman, Fran Gable." He stepped closer and ran his hand up and down her side. "Clyde and me been talking about Beef and wondering why he ain't here."

She clutched the rags tighter and stumbled to the back of the closet. "Ruby said he works in Morristown on Fridays. He's probably still working." Her voice was quiet and shaking.

Dewey threw his head back and laughed. "Working!" The liquor on his breath filled the small space. "I think your nigger son has something to do with him not being here."

She smiled, trying to ease Dewey's mind. "How could a little boy make a great big man do anything? You know Beef. He's found a game going on in Morristown and is good and drunk by now."

Dewey leaned closer. "Maybe." He breathed heavy on her and she held her breath. "You look good, Fran." He pulled her to him and pressed his body into hers. "You always look so good."

His voice was intense and strained and she felt panic rise to her chest. He covered her mouth with his and she tried to scream. He pulled her tighter and ripped open the back of her dress. She broke free and ran to squeeze past him. "Don't!"

He grabbed her arms. "Shut up when I'm talking, Fran!" He kicked the door shut and yanked her dress to the floor. She cried and covered herself with her arms. He yanked down the straps of her brassiere and pushed her against the wall, unbuttoning his pants. She tried to scream but Dewey forced his mouth over hers. She bit down on his lip and he flinched. When he saw blood on his hand he punched her hard in the belly. She groaned and doubled over. Dewey stepped toward her and she grabbed the galvanized bucket off the floor and swung it against his head. He struck her again, in the face this time, knocking her into the shelves. Another blow sent her falling hard to the floor and he kicked her in the stomach. She saw the light swinging above as she sank into darkness and then heard the thud of Dewey's body as it fell next to hers.

"Be still, Fran," Doc said, easing her back onto her bed. "Stay real still."

"Is the baby dead?" she asked. Helen and Loretta stayed at her side.

Doc listened long with his stethoscope and examined the bruises on her belly and face. "I believe the baby's okay. For now."

Her face tightened. "Don't let me lose it."

He held on to her hand. "Fran, the only thing I can do is tell you to be still in this bed until the baby comes. No washing, no milking, no working at the store."

I sat in the front room with Henry, Joe, John, and Milo. I still didn't know what happened and the wait for Doc was too long. "Henry, what happened to Mama?"

Henry glanced at Joe and shifted on the couch. "She got hurt."

"How?"

"A man knocked her over and she fell real hard."

"What man?"

"It don't matter, Jane. Sheriff Dutton's taking care of him."

I looked up at him. "It does too matter."

"Dewey Schaeffer did it."

"Why?"

"Because he was drunk and full of meanness."

I looked at Joe but he was studying a spot on his dungarees. "Did he *want* to hurt Mama?"

"He wanted what ain't his, Pretty Girl, and when he seen he wasn't going to get it he turned ugly and mean and hurt your mama."

I rested my head on his shoulder. Sometime later, when I was ready to know what Dewey wanted, I would ask Henry those questions.

Doc finished with Mama and walked into the front room. "Is the baby okay?" I asked.

"I don't know, Jane. But if your mama stays off her feet and stays still, maybe. I hope so. For now, just let her get some sleep. There's nothing broken."

Loretta and Helen closed the bedroom door and walked into the front room. "She's asking for you," Loretta said to Henry.

Henry opened the bedroom door and stuck his head inside. Fran waved him in and he sat on the chair next to her bed as he had so often done over the years, waiting it out with her. He looked down and rubbed his fingers along the inside seam of his pants. It was hard for him to look at her with her face and eyes swollen red and blue.

She watched him for the longest time. "Like old times, ain't it, Henry? You and Loretta coming over here, putting me back together again with bandages and salve."

"Them days are over, Fran. Sheriff Dutton's making sure that Dewey don't do this to nobody again." He laid his hand on top of hers. "I'm awful sorry, Fran."

She shook her head. "Ain't your fault, Henry. From day one I didn't want to have this baby. Now I don't want to lose it, but God seen my heart early on. You get what you deserve."

Henry shook his head. "I been around a long time, Fran, and from what I've seen God don't work that way. Good thing or else we'd all be in trouble." She was quiet. "There's just some sorry men in this world. But there's some awfully good ones, too."

"Sometimes it seems that Loretta married the last good one in Greene County."

Henry looked at the floor and cleared his throat. "Now that's enough of that talk."

"I've been in here studying on what happened—how I was in that closet with Dewey and then the next thing I know I'm here in my bed. And I have one question." He looked up at her. "Where in the world did you learn to hit like that?"

"I didn't . . ."

"Henry, the last thing I remember is smelling that god-awful perfume of yours." Henry slapped his head. "Now where did you ever learn to fight like that?"

"Five brothers and my sister, Sarah. She was meaner than all five boys put together."

"How many blows did Dewey take?" He held up two fingers. "Well, if I look like this, what does Dewey look like?"

"If his face feels anything like my hand then I suspect he looks pretty bad." He fidgeted with his hands and ran them up and down his legs. "Joe carried you out of there, Fran. When people heard the commotion they just poured into the hall but Joe ran right through them and covered you up. He had you out of there before I could think about it." He paused. "That about scared him to death."

"I reckon seeing two people laying there like that might scare anybody."

"He didn't care one iota that Dewey was laying there." She looked at him. "Fran, I've known both of you since you were little bitty and I might be getting old, but I still got eyes and I can still see that young boy from all them years ago when you two would walk up the hill to school together."

She turned to look out the window. "He's going back to Atlanta. That's where his work is."

He pulled her face toward him. "Do you think he'd drive all the way back here just to hear some singing when he could hear a dozen singers in Atlanta any time he wants?" She pulled away from him to face the window again and Henry knew she was done talking. "He's a good man, Fran." She closed her eyes, hoping he wouldn't say anything more. "Fran, you need . . ."

"I can't."

"He's not Lonnie."

"He don't deserve to be brought into this. He needs a good woman."

Henry sat on the edge of the bed and leaned over her, seeing that her eyes were wet. "Fran, that's you." She shook her head. "You been holed up in this house for so many years with Lonnie that you think being pushed down and stepped on is the best that it's ever going to get, but that ain't so." She looked out the window and Henry stood to leave, patting her shoulder. "Get some sleep, Frannie."

"Henry." He turned to her. "Why would he want a broken-down woman and four youngins that ain't even his? Why would any man want that?"

He stood by the door and shrugged. "I guess because twenty years from now he can't see his life without you all in it."

Loretta slept on the sofa and Henry laid a pallet on the floor beside her. He had just settled in when he heard a truck in the driveway. I jumped to the bedroom window and held my breath as Beef walked to our kitchen door. I looked at Milo and John but they were sound asleep. I wedged myself between their bed and the window so I could hear what was happening. Henry opened the door and stood on the porch with Beef.

"I heard what was done," Beef said.

"She's sleeping, Beef."

I pressed closer to the window, trying to ease it open. Henry walked with Beef to the driveway and I pushed the window up, leaning close to hear but I couldn't. I saw them in the moonlight and after several minutes Henry handed Beef something. Beef got into his truck and drove away. That was the last time I ever saw him. People said Beef just up and left without a word to Ruby or Louise. When people were at the store everyone speculated endlessly on why Beef left: *Couldn't live in a community with coloreds,* or *Couldn't bear to see his youngin go to school with a colored,* or *He came to his senses and knew Ruby and Louise would live in peace without him.* Everybody had their own theories but Henry never said a word.

Joe came to the house a couple of days later to ask Mama if we could go with them to the tobacco auction in Greeneville on Saturday morning. I groaned; I couldn't bear to hear how we'd get hit over the head but she didn't even think about it before she said yes. Henry went with us and Helen stayed with Mama for the day.

We walked into an enormous warehouse and gasped at the sight: The floor was covered with long rows of tobacco baskets holding some of the best-looking tobacco I'd ever seen. Joe led us to the rows where he and Del had unloaded their tobacco. Milo rested his hand on it. "That sure is some pretty tobacco."

"It's the prettiest we've ever had," Joe said. "No doubt about it."

The biggest tobacco companies at the time, such as Liggett & Myers, Philip Morris, R.J. Reynolds, and the Southwestern Tobacco Company, sent representatives to Greeneville to bid on the best of the crops. I watched as the reps meandered up and down the rows examining the leaves for damage and color. I grabbed Milo's hand as two of the men knelt beside the Cannon tobacco. An older man puffed on a pipe and grunted in the ear of the younger man with him. He took the pipe out of his mouth and stuck his nose into a basket. The man looked up at me and I smiled, squeezing tighter to Milo's hand.

"Is this your tobacco?"

"It's the Cannons'," Milo said. "And my mama and daddy's."

"Well, you tell the Cannons and your mama and daddy that they put out some real nice tobacco." Joe clapped Milo on the shoulder and we watched as he grew a foot right there in front of us.

The auctioneer made his way through the maze of tobacco and stood on a platform in the middle of the baskets. A man held up a number for the first lot that would be auctioned. I tried to understand what the auctioneer was saying but it was no use. The tobacco reps knew exactly what he was saying and they'd respond with a "hup" and a nod or a finger thrust into the air. Before we knew what happened Liggett & Myers had purchased the first crop of the day. We followed the crowd as the auctioneer moved down each row. The bids rolled in right on top of each other that morning as the men moved closer to the Cannon tobacco.

"Lot sixteen," the auctioneer said. "Lot sixteen." A man working with the auctioneer lifted a basket of the Cannon tobacco and walked it by the tobacco reps. Henry held on to me as the auctioneer rattled together a string of words I couldn't understand. "Hup," a rep from Liggett & Myers said. The warehouse buzzed with voices.

"Hup, hup," a man from Philip Morris said, raising his hand in the air.

"Hu-up." It was the rep from R.J. Reynolds. The auctioneer pointed at the rep, talking louder and faster than before.

"Hup!"

"Hey-up!"

My heart raced and I clung tighter to Henry's neck. "Hup," I said, yelling above the crowd. "Hup-hup."

The auctioneer stopped and turned to look at me. "Now how you gonna buy this tobacco?"

"I ain't wantin' to buy it. I'm wantin' to drive up the price." The crowd laughed and Joe lifted Milo onto his shoulders so he could see the men as they bid on his daddy's tobacco.

"Sold!" the auctioneer said, pointing to the R. J. Reynolds rep.

"What'd it get?" I asked Henry.

"It got 48.3 cents a pound," the auctioneer said. "You drove up the price for sure cause that tobacco brought in the highest bid of the day so far."

The Cannons' and Willie Dean's tobacco ended up getting the highest bid of the day—it brought in $565 per acre. Joe whooped and threw Milo into the air.

"Can we help you put out next year's crop?" I asked Joe.

His smile faded. "I won't be here next year. I need to get back to Atlanta."

I grabbed on to him. "No, Joe. Don't go back."

"I need to. I told them I'd go back once I got Mother and Pop's crop taken care of."

I held tighter to him. "When you leaving this time?"

He squeezed my shoulder. "I need to leave now but it'd be hard to go knowing one of my oldest friends is laid up in bed."

I smiled. "Then you'll wait till after the baby comes?"

"I'll need to make some calls to Atlanta. We'll see."

The next day Helen and Joe walked into Fran's bedroom. Joe handed her an envelope. "That's Milo's share of the money."

She opened it and took out a check made in her name. "No, Joe, this is your . . ."

"No, it's not our money. Willie Dean and Addy and Milo worked that tobacco. This is his money."

She stared at the numbers on the check. She'd never held something worth so much money in her life. "I don't feel right about taking this."

Helen sat beside the bed. "And we can't take it, Fran. He's gonna struggle enough. When his mama and daddy died it just opened up a whole world of struggle for him."

Fran looked at the amount on the check. "But there's more here than what the tobacco brought in."

Helen looked at her. "Fran, they ain't nobody here who's going to drink your money anymore. It's time you turned the electricity on in this house and got a wringer washer and a Frigidaire."

"I can't take what ain't mine."

"Then take it for Jane, John, Milo, and this new baby."

And she did.

I had been anticipating the first rehearsal for the Christmas pageant since the summer. I couldn't wait to run to the church each Saturday and practice, but before John, Milo, and I left that evening I jumped down the embankment and ran to Louise and Ruby's house. I pushed away the dead weeds and brush and climbed the hill to their door. Ruby answered. "Hi, Miz Ruby. Is Louise here?"

"I'll holler for her." I stepped inside and looked around the dingy room furnished with a tattered sofa and hardback chair setting up against a plastered wall with holes.

"Beef wasn't no-account at all," I said to myself. Louise came from the back of the house and smiled when she saw me. "We're fixing to go to the church for our first pageant practice." I left a space for Louise to respond but neither she nor Ruby did so I barreled on. "Loretta makes me play Mary every year but I've been studying on that and I believe it's time for somebody else to play her." Louise's eyes widened. "I believe you'd be perfect for it."

"I can't do nothing like that."

"They ain't a thing to it. Mary don't say nothing. She just sits there and holds the baby. Sometimes it's a live baby if one's been born but they ain't no new baby this year so you'll hold a winter squash." She gaped at me and then looked at Ruby. "You want to or not? We're fixing to leave."

"Can I, Mama?"

"That'd be something else," Ruby said. "You playing the mother of the baby Jesus himself." Ruby looked at me. "But we ain't never been to church."

I shrugged. "Then it's a good time to start, I guess."

Each morning that week Joe helped us milk the cows and take care of the animals and Helen made breakfast for us. Joe never went into Mama's room; he stood outside in the hallway and asked how she was doing. "I'm fine, thank you, Joe," she said day after day.

"I'm glad to hear it," Joe said, twisting his cap in his hands. My heart sank. My mother was too stubborn and Joe was too shy for anything to ever happen between them.

After our work was finished John and Milo and I ran off to school and left Mama alone in the house. Sometimes Helen stayed awhile and talked with her, or Loretta, Charlotte, or one of the women from church would come and clean and get supper cooked and put it in the warming compartment of the oven for when we got home.

When we got home from school John and Milo and I ran to her room and told her about what happened that day and listened to her stories of who visited and what they talked about with her. At night I slept with Mama, and John and Milo made a pallet on the floor of her bedroom. Looking back I know that it was during Mama's bed rest that we became a family. We talked way into the night about anything we could think of. "How's your book coming, Jane?" Mama asked.

She had never asked about my writing before. "I ain't writing it. I ain't able to do something like that."

She sat up. "If Henry can set down by that creek and tell one tall tale after another then you can sit down and write a book sure enough."

There was a faint note of belief in her voice that made me want to pop. I wanted to throw my arms around her neck but lay back on my pillow because none of us were ready for that.

• • •

For two days we painted magnolia branches in class. Each student brought in a branch from a tree off their property and we painted the great leaves a brilliant red or blue or gold. I painted several branches because I wanted to put them in Mama's room as decorations for Christmas. Miss Harmon helped us cut out and glue together tiny strips of construction paper that we formed into a chain. I made mine extra long so I could hang it around Mama's window in her room. Milo put the construction paper star he'd colored on Mama's headboard and John laid a small clump of hay on Mama's bedside, sticking three pinecones he'd painted in the middle of it. They were supposed to be Mary, Joseph, and Jesus but even if I squinted real hard I couldn't see any resemblance to people at all.

"Ain't this something," Mama said, over and over, admiring the decorations. "This is just some kind of pretty!"

"Joe's taking us out to shoot mistletoe," I said. "Then we'll hang that in here, too."

"Well, that will be something," she said.

"He said he'd help us bring in a Christmas tree, too, if that's all right." We waited, not knowing how Mama would react. We never had a Christmas tree as long as Daddy was living.

"That'd be fine as long as it ain't too much work for Joe."

"It ain't," John yelled, running from the room. Milo and I ran after him.

We were never more proud or excited than we were on that day, dragging that spindly pine tree through the Cannon pastures to Joe's truck. For the first time ever John and Milo and I were going to decorate a Christmas tree. In previous years Mama had always made sure that we got something in our socks that we hung on the mantel: an orange or some English walnuts, maybe a small bag of marbles or jacks. I didn't care about getting gifts this year. I just wanted to put up that tree and hoped it would bring some sort of peace to Milo and my mother. If ever there was a year for comfort and joy this was it.

We dragged the tree through the front door and laid it down in the front room. I ran into Mama's bedroom to tell her about it but realized she couldn't help decorate it. "You think you could watch us?"

"I bet old Doc would let me move out to the davenport." She lifted the covers and tried to move her legs but stopped.

"What's wrong, Mama?"

"Just sore."

I ran to the door. "Joe! You reckon you could get on in here and carry my mama out to the davenport?"

Mama waved in my direction as if swatting a swarm of bees. "Jane! What is wrong with you?"

Joe stood outside the bedroom door. "You reckon you could carry her so she can watch us decorate the tree?"

Joe twisted the cap in his hands. "You'd have to ask your mama that."

I looked at Mama and she was pale, her arm was over her face. "Mama, Joe'd carry you out to the davenport if you want."

"Lord have mercy," she said, muttering.

"Mama!" I said, louder. "Joe's waiting to carry you out to . . ."

"Okay, Jane. Okay!" She moved the blankets off her legs and straightened her house coat.

I turned to Joe. "Mama says okay."

"You doing okay, Fran?" Joe asked, walking close to her bed.

Mama wrapped a blanket around her shoulders, nodding.

"Holler if I hurt ya and I'll put ya back down." Joe put an arm under her legs and the other one under her back. She grimaced when he lifted her but I was the only one who saw it. Joe couldn't bring himself to look at her and she stared at the ceiling as he carried her through the hallway into the front room. He eased her down on the sofa and then backed away as if she was dynamite.

"Boy, that is some kind of tree!"

"Ain't it!" John said. "Me and Milo cut it down."

"Joe helped, too," Milo said, running around the tree to help Joe put it in the stand.

Once it was in place we strung popcorn and the berries from the mistletoe Joe shot out of the trees behind the Cannon house. Joe tried his best to string the popcorn but he was all thumbs. He kept at it, partly, I believe, because it kept him near Mama.

I stood back and marveled at the tree. Joe helped us cut a star out of two paper sacks, and John and Milo and I colored it with red and blue pencils. We glued the two stars together and then Joe lifted Milo so he could ease the star down onto the highest point of the tree. I jumped up and down along with John and Milo.

Mama and Joe laughed as they watched us and for a moment it felt like we were a family of sorts. I ran around the front room with John and

Milo and prayed that God would make a way for us to be a real family.

Margaret drove into our driveway late that afternoon. Fred Dog ran to greet her as he always did. She carried a pot of chicken and dumplings and I put it on the stove as she went in to see Mama, who was still on the sofa.

"Good to see you, Margaret," Mama said. Her voice was kind. Too kind, I thought.

"Ain't that a pretty tree! How you doing, Frannie?"

"I'll make it." My mother's voice was strange.

"Where's John and the little boy?"

"His name's Milo. You can call him by his name, same as everybody calls you by yours."

"I didn't mean nothing by it, Fran. I was . . ."

"Just dropping in to see how I was doing. I know." I stopped my work in the kitchen and crept through the hall to the front room, leaning close to the door.

"Of course I came to see how you're doing." Margaret's voice was tense.

"You didn't come to see me." I felt my heart pounding. What was my mother doing? "You ain't really been to see me in weeks. You used to come pulling up that driveway and your youngins would spill out of the truck so they could play in the barn with Jane and John. You ain't brought your boys by since Milo's been in this house because you're so afraid his colored skin might rub up against your boys."

"I wouldn't keep my boys from playing with your youngins."

There was a long pause. "I didn't say my youngins. I said Milo. You'll lean down and pet on that dog outside but you won't ever say a word to him." Margaret huffed but didn't respond. "I don't hear you denying it, Margaret."

I heard Margaret moving about. "You have lost your mind, Fran Gable. We've been friends since we were no bigger than John and you're . . ."

"Why'd you do it, Margaret?" Margaret stared long at her. "I don't care how you did it. You've always been smart. You were a whole lot smarter than me in school. You were smarter about who you married. I just want to know why you killed my cow."

"Lord help us all!" Margaret shouted.

"I know it was you, Margaret. I didn't at first. I thought it was Beef. Joe told me that Beef was too dumb and lazy to do something like that but I didn't believe him. For the rest of my life I would have thought it was Beef, but Ruby just happened to mention during that rainstorm that

Beef had been going into Morristown for work on Thursdays and Fridays. My cow died on a Friday. Since I've been laid up here for a week I've been studying on that and it's real curious to me. You know that dog barked and barked at Beef when he came here one day but he don't bark at you. If Beef had set foot on this property in the middle of the night I know Fred would have told everybody about it. But if you came, well, he'd just see a friend and lay right back down." My breathing had stopped. Margaret didn't move or attempt to say anything. "That sure was an awful lot of plotting and planning just to get rid of one little boy."

Margaret kept her back to Mama. "One little boy who ain't done nothing but bring trouble on you, Fran." She turned to her. "Your whole life ain't gonna be nothing but hardship."

"Could be. I ain't able to see into the future like you can. All I can do is what I'm supposed to do."

I leaned forward and could see Margaret looking out the window toward the tracks. "What now, Fran?"

"You can go home. Know that I forgive you here today for the trouble you caused and what you did to my cow. I know if I don't that I'll be eat up with meanness like you and that ain't no way to live. But that don't mean I have to call you my friend. I believe we're well past that now. I ain't saying nothing to Sheriff Dutton. Them boys of yours need a mama. So go on home where you belong and leave us alone." I ran and hid beside the chifferobe in the hallway and held my breath as Margaret passed. I could hear my heart in my ears.

Mama stood and walked to the door leading to the hall, leaning over to see me next to the chifferobe. She knew I'd been listening the whole time. She looked at me and I saw tears rimming her eyes. I nodded my head and she eased down the hall to her bedroom. This was our secret to keep.

Chapter
TWELVE

Our last night of practice for the Christmas pageant was three days before Christmas. We ate supper and, at Mama's insistence, left her alone in the house.

"But Henry could come stay with you," I said.

"Henry don't need to come down here and set with me. He's got enough to do. You all go on and act like you got some sense when you get there."

Loretta corralled the children into the church and Charlotte worked at finishing the last of the costume pieces: putting the foil from gum wrappers over the cardboard crowns of the wise men, trying different towels on the heads of the shepherds, and making sure that the sheet I wore as the angel wouldn't trip me as I declared the birth of Jesus.

Parts had been handed out at our first practice. John wanted to be a wise man. "I'm tired of wearing a towel on my head every year," he had said. In truth every child wanted to be a wise man, even the girls, because the wise men got to wear tin foil crowns and baking powder lids that had been painted gold to look like jewels. Loretta had read over notes she had scribbled onto the back of a stock sheet from the store. Alvin Dodson would play Joseph and Louise would be Mary. As suspected a winter squash had the part of baby Jesus. I was the angel and John and three other boys were the shepherds. Ned was the innkeeper. I knew the parts of the wise men would go to the older boys and girls; they always did so there wasn't a part for Milo.

Loretta peered over her glasses. "Delroy and Lyndon will be wise men and, Milo? Could you be a wise man this year?" That was our cast. We were a ragtag bunch but somehow I imagine that's probably what the crew from the first Christmas looked like.

At that last rehearsal I stood on a ladder and lifted my arms so the sheet would billow around me and addressed the shepherds who were kicking and punching each other in the arms. "Behold, you all, I bring good tidings . . ." The shepherds screamed and fell to the floor.

"You ain't been shot," Loretta said, running to the front of the church. "When you see the angel just look surprised and then get down on one knee to listen." I tried it again and this time only two shepherds fell to the ground. Those were pretty good odds to Loretta so she didn't stop us this time.

Charlotte dangled a cardboard star from a fishing pole over our heads and the three wise men followed it. Delroy Jenks reached up and smacked the star, making it loop around the fishing rod. "Don't touch the star, Delroy," Loretta said, yelling from the front pew. "They ain't nobody ever touched a star and lived. Not even a wise man." Charlotte untangled the line and the wise men came up the aisle again. "Walk like you're wise," Loretta said.

Milo led the way as he held the painted-red cigar box in his hands and concentrated on walking while pushing the crown up over his eyes. Charlotte ran to his side and sized the crown to fit. They walked to the stable (a few bales of hay and some milk cans) and bowed down in front of Alvin and Louise. "Keep the squash covered," Loretta said, pointing to Louise. "Wrap the blanket around it real good and pat it every now and again like a baby." Louise pounded the "baby's" back and the squash slipped right out of the blanket. Loretta ran after the rolling squash. "Don't let Jesus fall out of his swaddling clothes! That ain't nowhere in the Bible."

I took off my sheet and asked Loretta if I could go home to be with Mama. She nodded and I ran through the doors of the church. It would be dark before too long so I hurried along the tracks, practicing my line as the angel over and over until I got it right. I ran up the embankment and in through the kitchen door.

"I'm home," I said, throwing off my coat. She didn't answer. I walked toward her bedroom. "Mama. I'm home." I stepped into her room but she was gone. "Mama!" I shouted out to her in ringing tones that bounced back to me from the walls. I ran through the hallway and found her in the front room lying near the door. Her nightgown was wet with blood. I screamed and fell to the floor next to her. "Mama!"

"Run." Her voice was weak and thin.

I scrambled to my feet and ran toward the Cannons' as I had done so often over the last few months. Darkness was close and I ran faster. "*We done put enough people in the ground this year, Lord, and it seems to me you got plenty with you in heaven, so please don't let my mama and this baby die. Please save them.*" I burst through the Cannons' door. "Mama's bleeding!"

Helen grabbed her cane and used it to help her to her feet. "I'll call Doc." Joe grabbed my hand and ran with me to the truck. He sped away before I could close the door. We flew up our driveway and Joe ran to the house, throwing open the kitchen door.

"In the front room," I said, running behind him.

He leaned down next to her. "Fran!" He touched her face but her eyes were shut. "Fran!" Her eyes opened but grew heavy again. Joe scooped her up and carried her to the bedroom, easing her down on the bed.

"Why's she bleeding?" I screamed. "What's wrong?"

"I don't know, Jane. Run to the kitchen and put on some water to boil for Doc." My legs were numb. I couldn't find the pots. Where did we keep them? I threw open cabinet doors. "Please let them live," I said, over and over. I ran to the well and filled a large pot with water and threw it on the stove. Water spilled over onto the floor. I ran back into Mama's room.

"Stay with your mama, Jane," Joe said. "I'll fetch some towels and sheets."

I sat down next to her and started to cry. "Jane, listen to me." Mama's face was stricken and covered with sweat. "I know there's been times that I ain't been a fit mama to you and John."

I shook my head. "That ain't true, Mama. That ain't one bit true."

"I know I should have done more to get away from your daddy."

Tears fell down my face. "No, Mama. You couldn't have done any more."

"You tell John that you two are why I got out of bed every morning. You tell him that."

I ran my arm under my nose. "He's coming, Mama. He'll be here in a little bit."

Her back arched and she screamed, holding on to her belly. The sound terrified me and I jumped up, sobbing. She gasped, trying to catch her breath, and looked at me.

"Don't die, Mama. Please don't die."

The pain took her breath. "Don't cry, Jane." I nodded, wiping the tears away with my sleeve. "Be a big girl for John and Milo."

"Don't die, Mama," I said between sobs. I grabbed her hand and heard a door slam.

Doc ran into the room with Joe. "Jane! I need you to go wait in the kitchen for Henry and Loretta."

"I want to be . . ."

"Go, Jane!"

I left the room and Doc closed the door behind me. I slunk to the floor and put my ear against the door. All my life I'd heard people talk about the women they knew who had died in childbirth. Just four years earlier a young woman died and I heard the women talk about it at Henry's store. *Oh God, please! Please save my mama. Please save my mama.* Tears poured over my cheeks and I rubbed my face from one knee to the other, trying to dry them. I don't know how long I was there before Henry and Loretta came in with John and Milo. I reached for Henry and he picked me up as Loretta opened the door to Mama's room. Joe stepped out into the hallway.

"What's he doing?" I asked.

Joe looked frightened and small. "He's trying to help your mama." He didn't sound like Doc was doing much good.

"She was bleeding," I said. "Something's bad wrong."

"Doc's with her," Henry said, setting me down on the sofa next to John and Milo. "He's brought an awful lot of babies into this world."

"But what if the baby ain't supposed to be born? What if it's supposed to die like everybody else this year?"

"Shh, shh, shh. Don't talk that way."

Loretta flew from the room and in a flash ran back into it carrying things I couldn't see. A few minutes later we heard Mama scream and I grabbed Henry's hand. John burrowed next to his side and Joe held Milo on his lap. Another scream broke the silence in the front room and I covered my ears. *Please, please, please*, I whispered. *Please let them live. What will happen to us if my mama dies, too?* Pete and Charlotte arrived and joined us but no one said a word, not out loud anyway.

Pete stayed for a few minutes and then stood, putting a hand on Henry's shoulder. "I'm going to let folks know what's happening," he said. I watched as he left and my heart pounded. He knew my mother and the baby were bad off. Charlotte made coffee for the men and put peanut butter on saltines for everybody but nobody ate them.

Helen and Del arrived and when Helen heard

Mama screaming she rushed for the bedroom door. "Henry," she said, spinning on her cane. "Take these youngins to my house."

"No!" I shouted so loud that I startled myself. "I'm sorry, Miz Cannon, I don't mean to be smart mouthed, but I ain't leaving while my mama's in there."

"Me, neither," John said.

"Me, neither," Milo said.

She disappeared into the bedroom.

When Mama's groans and screams grew loud again Milo ran onto the back porch. Joe followed and picked him up. He was trembling and his eyes were as wide as the barn owl that perched in the rafters. "It's all right, Milo."

"My mama screamed." Tears filled his eyes and Joe held him tighter. "My mama screamed." Joe carried him into the backyard and stood at the top of the embankment. "She's dying." Words came in gasps. "I know how it sounds. I know how it sounds."

"She's screaming because there's a baby coming into this world." Joe was frightened but he made sure his voice was certain. "That baby has made up its mind and it's coming tonight." Joe sat on the ground and held Milo in his lap, waiting.

I slid my hand into Henry's. "She's gonna die, ain't she, Henry?"

"Your mama ain't once give up in her whole life." But his palm was sweaty. He stood and paced the room.

Two hours passed before Mama stopped screaming. After that we could hear her groan from time to time and then the hushed voices of Loretta, Helen, and Doc. Joe stood at the front window with Milo and John and looked out into the darkness. Time dragged on that night. We sat in that front room together for hours but no one moved with the exception of Henry to put more wood into the stove.

Sometime in the early morning hours Loretta opened the bedroom door and walked into the front room. She looked ragged but smiled, holding something wrapped in a blanket. John and Milo and I sprang to her side and she lowered the baby. "What is it?" I asked.

"Well, he ain't no winter squash."

"Is Mama gonna live?"

"Yes, but it'll take all of us watching after her for a long while."

Joe slipped past us and walked into Mama's room, looking at Doc. "How is she?"

"It was hard on her. The baby was turned and

didn't come easy. I had to break her pelvis." Blood-soaked sheets lay crumpled on the floor and Joe turned from them. "I clamped the bleeding before it filled her abdomen but she still lost a lot of blood. She's weak. She'll sleep for a good long time."

Joe sat by her bed and settled in for the night.

"The baby!"

Loretta stood up from the chair and held a finger to her lips. "He's fine, Fran." She pointed to a drawer that was setting on the floor lined with blankets. "He's been sleeping real good. How you feeling?"

"Like I been run over."

"It'll take you a long time to heal up, Fran, so you just rest as long as you need to." Loretta looked to the drawer. "He was bound and determined to get out into this world."

Fran smiled. "Addy said he'd be a fighter." She watched him sleep. "He's a pretty baby, ain't he?"

" 'Bout the prettiest one we've seen in Morgan Hill in a long time. He looks like his mama."

"Where's the youngins?"

"Out milking with Joe." Fran glanced up at Loretta. "He's been here all night. Sat right here in this chair and never moved." Loretta moved across the room. "Let me run get you something to eat. You need something to give you strength. Then you need to get some more sleep."

Loretta finished scrambling eggs when we tip-toed back into the house. "Your mama's awake," she said. John and Milo and I ran for the bedroom. "Don't you all wake that baby," she said, shaking the house with her voice.

Mama looked weak. The dark patches under her eyes were heavier than any time before. I'd never seen her look so sick.

"Did you see him?" I asked.

"I did."

"He's a fine-looking baby, ain't he?"

"He's mighty fine looking."

"What you gonna name him?" John asked.

"I don't rightly know."

"Well, we been thinking on it," I said.

"What have you come up with?"

I looked at John and Milo. "We like Willie Dean Henry Joseph Del Gable."

She smiled. "Well, he might end up turning on us one day if we call him all that. How about we call him Will Henry?"

John and Milo and I looked at each other and

smiled. Will Henry. Our brother. John and I ran to the kitchen to tell Loretta.

Milo stepped closer to Mama's bed and she smiled. "You ain't dying, ma'am?"

"No, Milo. Not yet, anyway."

He nodded and backed out of the room, making sure that she was breathing.

That night, all of Morgan Hill was going to be at the church to watch the Christmas pageant. Aunt Dora drove from Ohio to see Will Henry, and I threw my arms around her when she walked into the house. Helen said she would stay with Mama and the baby. Joe drove John, Milo, and me to church so we could get into our costumes. "Get back in the truck," Loretta said, handing my sheet to me. "We're taking the program to your mama."

Joe and Pete set up hay bales and put as many lanterns as they owned on the ground outside Mama's window, lighting our stage. The air was cold and clean, a fine winter's night for the program. I asked but Loretta wouldn't let Louise use Will Henry as the baby Jesus since he was brand new.

When people arrived they stood to each side of the manger bundled in their coats and holding lanterns; our little farm glowed in the light. Our breath made little puffs of smoke as we sang. Hoby Kane and Reverend and Mrs. Alden came from Greeneville to watch us, along with several members of the Mount Zion Baptist Church. Their voices boomed as we sang carols and I felt chills run down my spine.

Pete Fletcher announced the birth of Will Henry for those who hadn't heard and everyone cheered. Henry opened the window for Mama so she could hear the pageant; I couldn't see her looking out at us as she held Will Henry but I knew she was there. I stood on top of the hay bales and sang louder than I ever had because I wanted Mama to hear me. I wanted all of heaven itself to hear the children of the Morgan Hill Baptist Church sing about the birth of Jesus and for Willie Dean, Addy, and Rose to clap their hands watching us. It seemed that everybody had the same intention because that was the best pageant we ever performed and one of the best nights I can remember.

John was the first to wake on Christmas morning. "It's Christmas," he shouted, jumping up from the pallet. Will Henry jolted awake and cried. "Let's see if Santy's been here." John and Milo ran to the front room in their long johns. I was excited but I didn't run for the tree. I knew there wouldn't be any presents for us. I bent down and picked up the baby, wrapping the blanket around him. "He's been here," John shouted. "Santy's been here sure enough!" I ran with Will Henry into the front room and my mouth dropped. There were wrapped presents under the tree and lumps bulged in our socks that hung from the mantel. Milo and John crawled around the tree on their hands and knees trying to read the names on the four packages.

"I can't read this," Milo said, handing one of the presents to John. "What's this say?"

"Well, that's a *J* so this must be mine!"

I took the present from him. "That says Jane. That one yonder says John and that one there says Milo and this one's for Will Henry." John and Milo grabbed their presents and ran into Mama's room. I handed the baby to her so I could go get the socks down from the mantel. We dumped the contents of the socks onto the bed and screamed and laughed when we saw jacks and marbles and toy soldier figurines and some of the prettiest, roundest oranges we'd ever seen. Mama nibbled on some English walnuts that fell from one sock as John and Milo and I gobbled up chocolate drops from another.

"Whose gonna open their present first?" Mama asked.

"Milo should go first," I said. John agreed and Milo ripped open the brown wrapping and tore into the box inside. He pulled out a baseball and John shrieked when he saw it. Milo rolled it around in his hands as John broke into his package, mangling it in the process. He lifted a catcher's mitt from the box and both boys screamed.

"A gen-u-wine baseball and catcher's mitt," John said.

Mama unwrapped Will Henry's gift and pulled out a tiny blue coat filled with goose feathers. She ran her fingers over the stitching. "Who in the world?"

"You go, Jane," Milo said.

I slid my finger under the tape of the package so I could keep the wrapping and was careful as I opened each end. I lifted the lid of a cigar box and gasped when I saw a writing pad inside. "Now you can start your novel," Mama said. I picked up the writing pad and discovered the most beautiful book I'd ever held in my hands, black with gold leafing.

The Three Musketeers! I thought I had stopped believing in Santa long ago but I knew that Henry couldn't afford to buy so many gifts. Santa had to be real after all because if he didn't bring the gifts, who did? "How did Santa know?"

Mama smiled. "I think he must have lots of helpers," she said.

Helen and Loretta brought Christmas dinner to us; it took Henry and Del and Joe several trips to their trucks to unload all the food. Loretta sat Milo at the table and pulled an envelope out of her purse. She handed three photos to him. "Those are the pictures I took that day you caught all them fish. I forgot about the film and just now got it developed." I peered over Milo's shoulder and looked at the photos of him with Willie Dean, Addy, and Rose from that bright day in July. Willie Dean had a huge grin on his face and Addy and Milo were laughing. Rose was about to hug her daddy around the neck. Milo was quiet as he looked at the pictures. "I'm going to get some little frames for them so they won't get ruined," Loretta said. Milo never said a word. He held them throughout that day and when Loretta put them in frames a few days later, he draped Addy's locket over the top of one and set them all on the chest of drawers in the bedroom where they stayed till he was grown. They were the only family possessions he ever owned.

When Will Henry cried I bolted for Mama's room. Joe stood in the bedroom doorway and watched as John and Milo hovered over my shoulder as I carried the baby to the kitchen.

"Merry Christmas, Fran," Joe said, peering into the bedroom.

"Merry Christmas, Joe." He nodded and moved back into the hall. "Thank you, Joe," she said after him. He leaned back into the doorway. "Loretta told me you were the first one here to help when Will Henry was coming. And Henry said you carried me out of the schoolhouse and brought me home that night of the concert. I never thanked you." Joe twisted his cap in his hands and walked toward the chair by the bed, standing beside it. "It's all right. You can set with me."

They were both quiet for the longest time and when they did talk their conversation was awkward, filled with gaps and silences. "I know you stayed on long enough to see the baby come. Thank you."

"I didn't feel right about leaving with you laid up for so long."

She pulled her housecoat tight around her and rearranged the blankets covering her legs. "I imagine you'll be leaving for Atlanta soon."

They listened to the voices in the kitchen fussing over Will Henry. Joe cleared his throat and sat up in the chair. "Fran, I was a fool all them years ago." His voice was low.

She didn't look at him. "No, Joe. You weren't."

"I was a scared, backward boy and . . ."

"You don't have to say anything, Joe. I wouldn't have my youngins if things had been different."

They listened to the drumming of the bedside clock. During a lull she turned her head to look out the window. The ticking of the clock filled the room.

He bounced his leg up and down and pressed his hand down to stop it. "Fran." His voice was soft and she strained to hear him. "I don't want to go back to Atlanta. I've been on the phone with my buddy and his pop there for the last two weeks trying to put off going back because I just don't . . . All I do when I'm there is think about what's here . . . who's here. I work and see the faces of them youngins and I see yours and I can't stand it. Everything I want is right here." She kept her face to the window but tears filled her eyes. His leg bounced up and down again and he rubbed both hands into his thighs. "I may not be anything more than a farmer. Those twenty acres may be the only thing of value I'll ever own, but I'd be good to you." She didn't turn to look at him. "And I'd be good to them youngins." She remained motionless. "Fran, if you'd have me I'd help you raise your youngins as my own." The room was still. Her bad ear was toward him; he didn't think she had heard.

She turned and reached to touch his hand. She had.

It was a clear day in June when we gathered in the Cannons' backyard. The site where the Turner home was once located wasn't visible where we stood. A bank of clouds covered the sun but it was still beautiful under the great magnolia trees. Mama wore her best cotton dress, white with tiny pink flowers. Her face was soft and radiant, so different from the previous months. Joe beamed on that day. When I look back at the pictures they reveal that he was boyish and charming in a pair of dark pants and a crisp, white shirt and Mama was beautiful.

A year earlier Pete trembled as he conducted my daddy's funeral but now he looked confident as he officiated the marriage of my mother and father. I held Will Henry and stood next to Mama, and John and Milo flanked Joe, each of them holding one of his hands. It seemed fitting that we were holding a wedding on the Cannon property. The land that had taken a family was now offering up a new one.

I almost burst that day. God had heard my prayers and given us a daddy; He'd given all of us a family. As they repeated their vows the clouds moved from the sun and Henry and I both looked up into the sky, watching as light filtered through the leaves and scattered around us. Henry winked and I knew we shared the same thought. Willie Dean, Addy, and Rose were smiling.

EPILOGUE

I look out the window of the car and take in the sights that have changed so much over the years. My son drives past what used to be Henry's store and I turn in my seat so I can get a better look at it as we pass. I shake my head and groan. A neon sign hangs in the window announcing the latest videos available to rent. The gas pump has long been replaced with additional parking and the porch swing, coal burning stove, and cash register are all gone. My grandson Caleb squeals in his car seat and I turn and play with his feet. He is my fifth grandchild.

My husband, Al, and I have three children, two girls and a boy. Al is retired from the electric company in the town we live in forty miles outside Atlanta. We've been married for forty-four years.

John lives in northeast Ohio, just twenty minutes from Aunt Dora, who actually did meet a man on the bus. They married and had four children, eleven grandchildren, and are up to four great grandchildren. She's eighty-four now and still loves to kiss unsuspecting children. John spent a few years in the service before becoming a machinist in a factory. He and Edie have two children and five grandchildren and, although he complained about it each spring when we were growing up, he still puts out a garden every year, growing some of the finest tomatoes I've ever seen.

Will Henry was a sweet baby and I often wondered what our home would have been like without him. He settled in Knoxville and he and his wife have two children and are expecting their first grandchild any day.

My parents had two children together, David and Paul, and though I was married and gone when they were both still little boys, they have been fine brothers, living in Nashville and Kentucky with their families.

Milo stayed closest to home, marrying a woman named Clara and settling in Greeneville, where he works as an insurance adjustor. He has four children and seven grandchildren. Milo looks just like Willie Dean and one of his daughters is the spitting image of Addy in that spring of '47. He visits our parents often and we talk a couple of times a week on the phone about how they're doing. It took him a year before he stopped calling Mama "ma'am." He started calling her "Mother" and still does to this day. While growing up I know that life was difficult for him at times and during those periods he'd run off to be by himself somewhere. He always told Mama where he was going and he'd run up into the hills or sit by the creek; I imagine he used that time to try to see his daddy's face or hear his mama's laugh. My mother kept her promise to Addy and loved Milo like one of her own. She never treated him better or worse than the rest of us. If we were out and about and someone would see Milo and inquire who he was, she would simply say, "He's my son." And she meant it.

Mama and Dad are old now. My mother has arthritis but she still makes biscuits and gravy on

Sunday morning for breakfast. Dad and the boys worked the farm after I left but Dad took a job as a land assessor for the county to help pay the bills. He retired seventeen years ago.

My grandma Helen died when I was seventeen and grandpa Del died two years later, the same year I got married. Mama and Dad moved into the Cannon house after that and finished raising the boys there. It was during that move that I discovered all the letters my father had received from Morgan Hill when he was overseas. I skimmed through the letters and stopped when I recognized my own poor penmanship.

Dear Joe, I hope your good. It's hot here. Is it hot ther? What do you eat ther? Last night we had beens and cornbread. Well, bye. Your frind, Jane.

I picked up another stack of letters and found one that was folded into a small square. I was careful as I opened it so the creases wouldn't tear. I looked at the signature. It was from my mother, written a year after Joe left.

Joe, I hope you are good and staying warm. Gloria B. had a baby, a girl they named Hope. Hubert J. died. He was 74. Not much else new. We're good here. Jane is four and John's almost two. They're good youngins. I wish I could do more for them but my hands are full with so much. I can't look back over what might have been, though. They need a mama. I hope you're eating good. I think and pray for you often. Love, Fran

I ran my fingers over the thin paper and my eyes filled. He must have folded the letter and kept it in his pocket during the war. He always loved her.

I rummaged through another box and found all the medals he'd earned and the letters from grateful parents or spouses who lost a son or husband in the war. I pored over those letters and tried to imagine my dad when he was overseas. I can still remember him as he returned from the war and the first Sunday he came back to church. I didn't think he looked anything like a hero but I was wrong. The medals at the bottom of the box proved that he was but no one ever knew it. That's the way he wanted it.

I filtered through the box and found articles from newspapers that Helen had saved and a document from the War Department. *Three gunshot wounds.* I read further. *Uncommon valor. Conflict at Normandy.* We had heard about Normandy on the radio at Henry's but never imagined Dad was there. I carried the box in to Dad who was packing things in another room. John and Milo and the boys gathered around it, looking at the medals. Dad was quiet as he thumbed through the letters.

He received the Purple Heart and Congressional Medal of Honor, but even those were put away in the box. I asked Dad if I could have the medals and letters after he was gone and he handed them to me that day. "I don't need to read them again," he said. "I remember. I've always remembered."

In all my years I never thought of Dad as a hero of the war but heroic in the sense that he took all of us in. That was uncommon valor. On that day I realized that he was a hero in every sense of the word. He is the bravest man I've ever known.

I glance over where Henry and Loretta's house used to stand. Someone tore it down and built two duplexes in its place. In 1980 I was washing dishes when the phone rang in our home. "You better come now if you want to see him." I called Al and asked him to pick up our youngest child from school and jumped into the car.

Please let me get there, I prayed. *Please let me see him one last time.* I pulled into the parking lot at the hospital in Knoxville and ran up the stairs to Henry's room. Mama, Dad, Loretta, and Henry's children were in the hallway.

"He hasn't responded in two days," Loretta said. "I just don't want you to get your hopes up."

I nodded and stepped inside the room. Henry had had a stroke a month earlier and by all appearances it'd seemed he was well again until a heart attack had put him back in the hospital four days before. I walked over to his bed and looked at him. His face was lined with eighty-six years of wrinkles and the skin on his hands was thin and marked with age. I slid my hand under his and held on to it as tears streamed down my face. I bent close to his ear. "I'm here, Henry."

His eyes fluttered open. "Hey, Pretty Girl."

His voice startled me and I laughed, tears rolling over my nose. I wiped them away with the back of my hand. "Just where do you think you're going?"

"Fishing."

I held his hand between both of mine. "Sounds boring."

"You ain't ever been fishing in heaven. Fish come right up out of the water smiling at you." I laughed and cried harder. "Where's that book you were going to write?"

I shook my head. "I'm getting too old now. I don't even know what to write about."

"Just write about things close to home. And if I'm in it don't forget to tell everybody how good looking I am."

I nodded and tears fell onto his bed. "I wish you'd stick around so you could see it."

He squeezed my hand. "I'll see it, Pretty Girl. Don't you worry about that."

I leaned down and kissed his face. "Thank you, Henry. You were the father that I didn't have for . . ."

He tried to squeeze my hand but he didn't have the strength. "The blessing was mine, Pretty Girl. Every single blessing was mine."

Loretta asked me to say the eulogy at Henry's funeral and the church was packed. *When I was a little girl,* I said, *my best friend was a fifty-three-year-old man named Henry Walker. And I don't know what I would have done without him. He had a hard time saying no to people and some probably took advantage of that. He wasn't the greatest businessman in the world; he did a lot of things wrong. But he did a whole lot more things right. He offered friendship and grace to everyone around him and because of him Morgan Hill became a community of hope for everyone who* lived here. He kept a quote on the side of his cash register that said, "Character's found in how you treat people who can't do anything for you." I once asked Henry what that meant and he said, "I guess it means just take care of people." And that's what Henry did. Every day. He took care of others and let his life speak for him as simply as the birds of the air and the lilies of the field. I spoke a few minutes longer, sharing some of my favorite stories about Henry, and everyone laughed. He would have loved that. *You have fought the good fight, Henry. You have kept the faith, finished the race, and lived out your dash with honor and dignity.* I looked out into the faces of friends and family and smiled. *I am thankful today. I am thankful for a man named Henry that God sent to a place called Morgan Hill.*

When I was nine years old I dreamed of being part of a real family and that dream came true. It wasn't easy bringing up a black boy in a white home but we did what we could. We fought and argued and drove each other crazy at times but we all survived. I like to think that maybe we even thrived because we learned how to rely on each other and God. There are more stories to tell but I'll leave those to Milo and John.

My son, Aaron, turns into the drive and I can

see Mama and Dad sitting on the front porch. Dad stands when he sees the car and waves. Mama eases to the steps of the porch where she waits for us. Aaron lifts three-year-old Ashley from her car seat and I unbuckle a crying Caleb from his.

"Good grief! What's all that noise for?" I ask, kissing his face.

"Is that the new grandbaby?" Mama asks, walking to us.

"Well, he ain't no winter squash." I hug my mother and put Caleb in her arms.

"Ain't he a pretty something! Look how pretty, Joe."

Dad rubs his rough finger across Caleb's face and he smiles up at them. "You can call me Pap. All the other grandbabies do."

Aaron hands Mama a card. "Happy Mother's Day, Grandma. I wanted to get you something so I thought we could go into Greeneville and I could buy you a new outfit."

She shakes her head. "I don't need a thing. I got this new grandbaby. That's all I want."

I hand her a bouquet of flowers. "Those are from Al. We dropped him off at the nursing home in Greeneville so he could see his mother. Milo's going to get him later for supper and bring him back here with his family."

"How is Alvin?"

"He's good, Mama."

Alvin Dodson went into the army for two years when he graduated from high school and when he came back to Morgan Hill he was different. He was a man. I could no longer remember the little boy who'd rubbed cockleburs into my hair.

Mama and Dad coo at the baby and Caleb kicks his legs, smiling. They laugh, watching him. Aaron plays with Ashley in the yard and she holds on to his hands and climbs up his legs. In my mind's eye I can still see Willie Dean lifting Rose to his shoulders the day I met them. Ashley climbs as high as she can and Aaron throws her into the air. "Lift me higher, Daddy." He holds her higher and she stretches her arms toward the sky. "Higher, Daddy. Lift me higher so I can touch the angels." He puts her on top of his shoulders and I smile. When I was a child I never had to stand on anyone's shoulders to touch the angels around me.

They were always within reach.

Read on for an excerpt
from the new book by
DONNA VANLIERE

The
Christmas Promise

AVAILABLE IN HARDCOVER FROM ST. MARTIN'S PRESS

*I still think that the greatest suffering
is being lonely,
feeling unloved, just having no one. . . .
That is the worst disease that any
human being can ever experience.*
—Mother Teresa

I peeked through the kitchen drapes that morning and rushed to grab a bucket and rag. *Looks like a nice one,* I said to myself, straining to see out the window. Someone had left a refrigerator in my driveway. I squeezed dishwashing liquid into the bottom of the bucket and filled it with warm water, splashing my hand till it disappeared in suds. I tied up my running shoes—the sassy pink neon ones with the green stripes—and slipped a bottle of household cleaner into my coat pocket. A blown porch light stopped me on the steps and I looked up at it. "Good grief. That bulb didn't last very long. I need to get one of those bulbs that last a year." I stepped into the kitchen and reached to the top shelf of the utility closet. Back on the porch, I unscrewed the old bulb from the bottom of the light casing. "There you go," I said, screwing in the new one.

I turned to the refrigerator in the driveway, sizing it up. "Not too big. Twenty cubic feet, I'd guess." I opened the door and backed away, holding my hand over my nose. "I'll have you cleaned and find a new home for you by lunchtime," I said, slipping on a pair of bright yellow latex gloves. I was used to talking to myself; I'd been a widow for seven years. I was never concerned about talking to myself; what worried me is how I answered myself, and I was *really* troubled when I argued with myself! I pulled out one shelf after another, soaking my rag and scrubbing at unrecognizable globs of petrified food. I sprayed down the inside and tackled the back wall with a vengeance.

"There *is* a junk law, you know!" I cringed at hearing that familiar voice and closed my eyes. Maybe if I couldn't see her she wouldn't actually be there. "The city has mandated codes." I scrubbed harder. "Gloria Bailey, I'm talking to you."

How I despised that tone. I took a breath and

lifted my head to see my neighbor standing on the other side of her fence. "Good morning, Miriam."

"Gloria, does anyone ever bother to let you know that they're dropping this rubbish off?"

I shoved my head inside the fridge, scrubbing at the walls. I once told my friend Heddy that there wasn't enough room in the cosmos for Miriam's ego. Her affected British accent was as real as her blond hair and her name. Miriam Lloyd Davies. Come on! "It'll be gone by noon, Miriam," I said, wringing out the rag.

"I doubt it, by the looks of it," Miriam said. "But if it's not gone I'll need to have it hauled out of here. I don't pay taxes to live next to a junkyard."

It's amazing how perfect your posture becomes when you've been insulted. Every vertebra in my back straightened to supreme alignment as I walked up the driveway. "I don't pay taxes to live next to a junkyard!" I said, whispering.

When I moved into my home six years ago a lovely young couple with two small children lived in the house next door. They were always polite, smiling and waving each day, even leaving a present on my doorstep each Christmas. If my work annoyed them, they never showed it. Miriam moved in three years ago when the young couple found themselves expecting a third child and in need of a larger home. She was graceful and statuesque—fitting for a stage actress and professor's wife—but I found her to be cold and distant, although her husband, Lynn, was always gracious and warm. Lynn died a year after moving into the home. I tried on several occasions to befriend Miriam, assuming our widow status would assure some sort of bond between us, but just because someone is plopped into your life doesn't mean a friendship will be forged.

I often felt pasted together, compared to Miriam's refined look. I looked my age (sixty and proud of it) while Miriam denied hers (fifty and holding). I've never been what you could call fashionable, but I take pride in my appearance. I like my clothes to match and am most comfortable in cotton and jersey (but no belts). I don't wear anything that hurts! Miriam preferred slacks with a designer blouse or cashmere sweater and she was always neat, nothing disheveled about her. Her hair was the color of golden honey and framed her face in a chic bob. She promptly made her next appointment at the beauty salon for five weeks to the date of her last cut and coloring. My hair was salt and pepper (more salt than pepper) and hung in soft, or rather, annoying curls around my face. When it got too long I simply bobby-pinned it back until I found the time to give myself a trim.

I walked into the kitchen and dialed a number on the phone, listening as it rang in my ear. I was about to hang up when the line clicked on the other end. "Hello! Heddy?" I said. "I've got a fridge. Can you look through the list and see who needs what?"

I heard Heddy rustling through papers. Dalton Gregory was the retired school superintendent and his wife, Heddy, was a nurse at the hospital who was on duty when I had my gallbladder taken out four years ago. *We've been taking stuff from you ever since,* Heddy once said. I couldn't do my work without them. They had the organizational skills that I sorely lacked. I relied on sticky notes and miscellaneous paper scraps to remind myself of appointments or calls, and my idea of filing was stacking things on the kitchen table. Dalton and Heddy kept everything on computer and could pull it up with the touch of a finger. I still wasn't entirely sure how to turn on a computer.

"A family with three children called yesterday," Heddy said. "Their refrigerator broke four days ago and the father is in the hospital. The mother hasn't had any time to look for a new one."

I peered through the drapes and watched Miriam nosing around the refrigerator. I shook my head, watching her. "Can Dalton come pick it up and deliver it?" I rapped on the window and Miriam jumped, making me laugh. She threw her nose in the air and marched to her own yard. "Sooner than later, Heddy. Miriam Lloyd Snooty Face is riding her broom again."

Years earlier, I had been driving home late one winter night when, near the downtown bridge, I noticed a homeless man with a red hat who wasn't wearing socks with his shoes. I couldn't get the image of the man out of my mind. What if that had been my own son? Would anyone have helped? Days later I walked into Wilson's Department Store and found socks for ninety-nine cents a pair in a discount bin at the back of the store. "What would it cost if I bought the whole bin?" I had asked owner Marshall Wilson.

"Tell you what," Marshall had said. "I'll donate all these *and* hats and scarves to your cause." I hadn't realized I was championing a "cause," but when I delivered the clothes out of the back of my trunk I knew that the cause had found me. People needed help right in my own backyard. I had been slumping around and feeling sorry for myself long enough and needed to do something about it.

"Thank you, Miss Glory," the man with the red hat had said. The name Miss Glory stuck. Since that time I'd taken in whatever I could get my hands on and given it out to the homeless and families in need, especially young single mothers with children. My husband and I had four children and I couldn't imagine having raised them by myself.

I taught cooking in my home along with simple classes like how to make a budget and basic child care. Dalton taught computer and job interviewing courses, but all our classes were small. I didn't have the space in my house for large groups.

"He'll be there in a bit," Heddy said. "Then Miriam won't have anything to complain about."

"I doubt *that*," I said.

"Gloria?" Heddy's voice changed and I wondered what was wrong. "We got word that Rikki Huffman was charged with drug possession last night."

I fell into a chair at the kitchen table. Rikki was a single mom I'd been working with for the last two years who seemed to be getting her feet on the ground. "No! She was doing so great. Where is she?"

"They have her at County." Heddy was quiet. "She'll spend time in jail with this offense, Gloria." I assumed that, but still hoped Heddy would say something else. "Are you all right?"

"Not really," I said, rubbing my head. "Who has her kids?"

"DFS. The Department of Family Services will place them. Maybe they already have. You've done everything you could for Rikki. You know that, right?"

I sighed. "My mind knows that, sure."

"Rikki just can't break the cycle," Heddy said. I was quiet. "Gloria? Gloria!"

I jumped at her voice. "Yes."

"Don't blame yourself." That always proved to be easier said than done for me. "You can't save everyone. It's not your job."

I hung up the phone and sat at the table, thinking about Rikki for the longest time. I nursed a cup of coffee before heading back outside.

"I'm going on holiday for five days, Gloria."

I turned to see Miriam behind the fence. That sounded wonderful to me. After learning about Rikki's arrest I wasn't in the mood to have Miriam breathing down my neck at every turn. "That's great," I said. "It's always good for you to go away." That didn't come out right. "I mean, good for you to leave." I was making it worse, and put on the most sincere fake smile I could muster.

"It's my birthday," she said. "My daughter and her family have asked me to celebrate with them. One only turns fifty once, you know!"

A loud gust of air shot over my teeth before I could rein it back in. "Ha!" Miriam's eyes narrowed, looking at me. "Fifty! Well . . . congratulations . . . *again*," I added, under my breath.

"Would you watch the house for me?"

"Of course," I said.

"Just keep an eye open and notify the police if anyone drops off any unsightly rubbish."

I cringed. It was really hard to like that woman.

The bus was packed that morning. Several people had shoved their backpacks up against the window to eke out a few minutes of sleep between stops. Twenty-four-year-old Chaz McConnell sat next to a fat man who was somehow under the impression that he had rights to Chaz's seat as well. Chaz spent the majority of the ride claiming his armrest and foot space while watching the snow fall outside.

The bus drove through the town square and

pulled in front of the bus stop, which was nothing more than a small storefront a few blocks from town with a bench in front of it. Chaz grabbed his backpack and inched his way out of the seat; the fat man never bothered to get up. Chaz pulled the hood of his sweatshirt up and saw apartments just up the street. A one-bedroom apartment was available and he could move in after he paid a one-month deposit and the first month's rent. He pulled out a wad of money and walked into the apartment with everything he owned stuffed into a backpack. Later in the day he saw a futon and its frame by the Dumpster and made his way across the parking lot to check it out. He noticed that the owner of the house across the road was replacing Christmas lights on the trees in front of his home.

"Those lights have been up all year," a neighbor woman said when she saw Chaz looking at them. "They keep them on all the time." The neighbor woman kept talking about the lights but Chaz ignored her, examining the futon frame. One leg was broken but he knew he could just prop it up on something and have a suitable bed. He dragged it up the three flights of stairs to his apartment and put it against the pale beige wall in the bedroom. Days later he found a small black-and-white TV with poor reception by the Dumpster, and a few days after that a card table. He used milk crates as chairs for the table and drawers for the few clothes he owned. As far as he was concerned, he had all the furniture he needed.

When Chaz started the walk to Wilson's Department Store on Monday it was barely drizzling, but when he approached the town square there was a deluge. The streetlamps had been wrapped with evergreen and topped off with red bows. Several of the storefronts were decorated for the Christmas season, including the barbershop, which had managed to put a waving Santa in the front window to announce the special cut and shave of the week. When he passed the church on the square, several people were coming out of the basement and darting for their cars. He meandered between them and pulled the hood of his sweatshirt over his head, making a dash for the entrance of Wilson's. It was busy inside, but that was to be expected right before Thanksgiving. He took off his sweatshirt and held it away from himself, running his fingers through soggy hair.

"Good morning," a sales associate said behind a stack of ladies' sweaters she was carrying. "Can I help you find anything?"

"Mr. Wilson told me to come in this morning to fill out paperwork for a job."

"The office is just up the stairs behind the purses." The stack of sweaters tumbled to the floor but Chaz ignored them, walking past the salesgirl toward the small flight of stairs. The store was old: As he looked at the elevators, his guess was it dated back to the early 1950s, but they'd done a lot of remodeling over the years. The floor on the main aisle was made of bright white tiles. The cosmetics and jewelry counters faced each other on the main aisle, and oversized lit Christmas stars and bulbs dangled from the ceiling above each counter. The men's and women's departments were on either side of the main aisle, with carpeting in shades of burgundy and green. Beyond the cosmetics counter were shoes and ladies' handbags, and the stairs leading to the office.

Chaz took the stairs by two and found the small office. A woman wearing a red sweater covered with green and silver beaded ornaments was on the phone. She had a small sign on her desk that read JUDY LUITWEILER. "I'm sorry," she said when she hung up the receiver. "My daughter's having a baby any day now and I keep calling her. Anxious grandma, you know!" She spun her hands in the air and Chaz tried to smile but was too wet to care.

"I'm supposed to start work today. They told me to come up here for the paperwork."

"Sure. Sure," Judy said, opening a metal file drawer behind her desk. "What's your name?"

"Chaz McConnell."

She rifled through the files like a squirrel after a nut. "And which department will you be in?"

"Security."

"Sure. Sure," she said, pulling a manila folder from the cabinet. "Do you have any children?" she asked, sorting the papers. "We love children around here."

"No, I don't."

"Morning, Chaz." Marshall Wilson stepped down from the office behind Judy's, wearing jeans and a denim shirt. "How are you, son?" No one had called Chaz son in years and the word sounded odd to him.

"Fine. How are you?"

"Better than I deserve to be at my age, I'm certain of that," Marshall said. "Did you get settled into a place?" Chaz nodded. "We're ramping up for a busy Christmas season, so we're glad you're here."

"You must be Chaz." Chaz turned to see a black man dressed in dark pants and a gray shirt with a badge attached to the left side of his chest pushing his way into the cramped office. The man stretched out his hand and Chaz wiped his off on his jeans before shaking. "I'm Ray Burroughs. I'll be training you." Chaz summed him up: He was about his size, maybe a little heavier, but he knew he was going to look as dorky as Ray did in that uniform. "Come on down to the office. You can fill out the papers there and get something dry to put on."

Chaz followed as Ray ran down two flights of stairs to the break room. He pointed to the time clock on the wall. "Clock in here when your shift starts." He took the card with Chaz's name on it and handed it to him so he could punch in, then led him down the hall. He glanced down at Chaz's soggy shoes. "Did you walk here?"

"Yeah."

"Don't you have a car?"

"I did. It was stolen a couple of months ago." The truth was, Chaz had owed some small gambling debts to a guy a few towns ago and the man had taken the car as payment. Chaz didn't care; he thought it was a piece of junk anyway.

"Are you going to walk to work every day?" Ray asked.

"Yeah."

"Then you'd better invest in an umbrella." The top of the office door was etched glass. The word SECURITY was written in black block letters in the middle of the window. They stepped inside. The walls were brick, but someone had painted them off-white. Four video monitors sat on the large desk in the center of the room with images from select departments in the store. Ray pointed to a black vinyl sofa against the wall. "You can sit there if you want, or here at the desk. It doesn't matter." Chaz looked at the desk covered with papers, files, and cups of old coffee, and opted for the couch. Ray sat on the wooden swivel chair at the desk and leaned back. The thick spring whined beneath him. "So, word is that Mr. Wilson hired you away from another store?"

"That's right," Chaz said, filling out the first line.

"How long did you work security there?"

"I didn't," Chaz said. "I stocked shelves."

"Then how'd you get hired for security?"

Chaz had been living in a town an hour away when he met Marshall Wilson. For the first time in his life he was working in a retail store rather than in a restaurant as a waiter or cook. Chaz was stacking men's jeans in cubbies that stretched to the ceiling when Marshall needed assistance, but Chaz wasn't paying attention—his eye was on a young woman pushing a baby stroller. The baby was asleep and the woman was discreet as she first put a pair of pants and then a sweater into the bottom of the stroller, covering the items with the baby's blanket and diaper bag. "You forgot a belt to go with that outfit," Chaz whispered as he moved past her toward his cart filled with denim. Her back stiffened as she flung the goods onto the clothing table in front of her and fled the store. The baby never wakened. Chaz laughed as he watched her and climbed back onto the ladder to replenish the top row of jeans.

"You handled that well," Marshall said.

"Thanks," Chaz said without looking down.

"Would you be interested in changing jobs?"

Chaz stacked four pair of jeans into the top cubby. "Nope."

"I need another security guard at the store. I'm sure it pays better than what you make here."

Chaz looked down and saw an elderly man with white hair wearing jeans and a red plaid flannel shirt. *Probably owns a hardware store,* Chaz thought. "I'm listening," he said, shoving the pair of jeans he had wedged under his arm on top of the stack.

A full-time job sounded good to Chaz at that point. *There's a great cure for being broke,* his mother used to say. *Go to work.* He didn't like to stay in one place too long and was ready for a change. Chaz was always ready for a change. With every move he'd think, *Okay, this time I'll do better. I'll be better. I'll change.* But he never did. He couldn't. But this time he really thought he could make it stick, so he packed his bags.